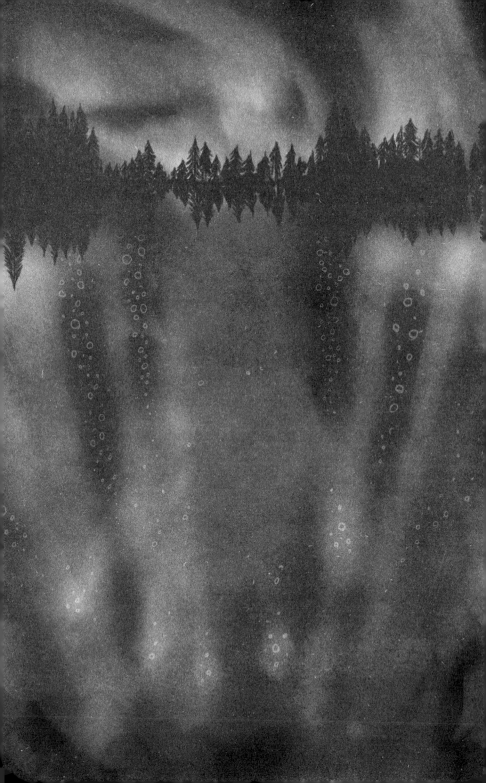

For everyone who's ever felt alone

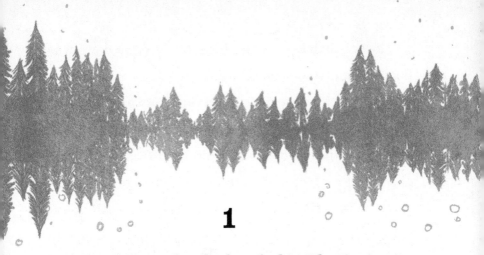

1

Until last summer I thought the only thing I had in common with that whale on the beach was a name.

I sat with Grandpa after collecting shells and driftwood scattered along the shore, and wildflowers from the dunes. The shells and driftwood were for Grandma, and the flowers were for the whale. Grandpa had asked how school was going, and I told him it was the same, which wasn't good. I'd been at that school for two years and still felt like the new kid.

Grandpa patted the sand next to him. *"Did you know she was probably deaf too?"* he signed.

I didn't have to ask who he meant. The whale had been buried there for eleven years, and my parents had told me enough times about what happened that day.

I shook my head. I hadn't known that, and I didn't know why Grandpa was changing the subject. Maybe he didn't know what to tell me anymore about school.

The whale had beached herself the same day I was born. When she was spotted in the shallow waters of the Gulf, some people stood on the shore and watched her approach. My grandma ran into the cold February water and tried to push her away from land, as if she could make a forty-ton animal change her mind about where she wanted to go. That was really dangerous. Even though the whale was weak by then, one good whack with a tail or flipper could have knocked Grandma out. I don't know what I would've done— jumped in like she did or just stood there.

"She wasn't born deaf like we were," Grandpa continued. *"The scientists who studied her said it had just happened. Maybe she'd been swimming near an explosion from an oil rig or a bomb test."*

When Grandpa told a story, I saw it as clearly as if it were happening right there in front of me. His signing hands showed me the whale in an ocean that suddenly went quiet, swimming over there, over there, over there, trying to find the sounds again. Maybe that was why she'd been there on our Gulf of Mexico beach instead of in deep ocean waters where she belonged. Sei whales didn't swim so close to shore. Only her, on that day.

"A whale can't find its way through a world without

Library of Congress Cataloging-in-Publication Data
Names: Kelly, Lynne, author.
Title: Song for a whale / Lynne Kelly.
Description: First edition. | New York : Delacorte Press, 2018. | Summary:
Twelve-year-old Iris and her grandmother, both deaf, drive from Texas
to Alaska armed with Iris's plan to help Blue-55, a whale unable to
communicate with other whales.
Identifiers: LCCN 2018006061 | ISBN 978-1-5247-7023-5 (hc) |
ISBN 978-1-5247-7024-2 (glb) | ISBN 978-1-5247-7025-9 (ebook)
Subjects: | CYAC: Deaf—Fiction. | Whales—Fiction. | Automobile
travel—Fiction. | Grandmothers—Fiction.
Classification: LCC PZ7.K29639 Son 2018 | DDC [Fic]—dc23

The text of this book is set in 11.5-point Eames Century Modern.
Interior design by Maria T. Middleton

Printed in the United States of America
10 9 8 7 6 5 4 3 2 1
First Edition

LYNNE
KELLY

SONG
FOR A
WHALE

Delacorte Press · New York

SONG FOR A WHALE

sound," Grandpa added. *"The ocean is dark, and it covers most of the earth, and whales live in all of it. The sounds guide them through that, and they talk to one another across oceans."*

With the familiar sounds of the ocean gone, the whale was lost in her new silent world. A rescue group came to the beach and tried to save the whale, and they called her Iris. Grandma asked my parents to give the name to me, too, since I'd entered the world as the whale was leaving it.

After the marine biologists learned all they could from her, she was buried right there on the beach, along with the unanswered questions about what had brought her to that shore.

We lived on that coast until the summer after second grade, when my family moved to Houston for my dad's new job. Since then, we went back just once or twice a summer. The good thing about our new home was that it was closer to my grandparents. I liked being able to spend more time with them, especially since they were both Deaf like me. But we all missed the beach, and I missed being around kids like me. My old school had just a few Deaf kids, but that was enough. We had our classes together, and we had one another.

"But it's different for us," Grandpa signed. "Out here, there's more light, and all we need is our own small space to feel at home. Sometimes it takes time to figure things out. But you'll do it. You'll find your way."

I wish I'd asked him then how long that would take.

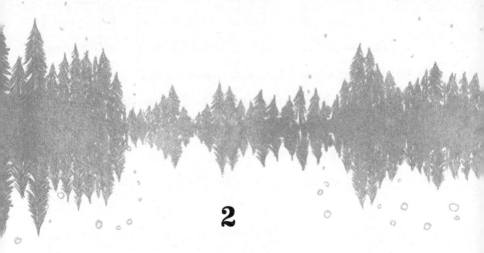

2

I'd come to the conclusion that sending me to the office was Ms. Conn's only joy in life. That made me responsible for her happiness, in a way, but I tried to slip into class without her noticing. I was only a minute late this time, and I had a really good reason.

She pointed toward the front office before I could drop into my chair.

When I got back to the room with my tardy pass, Ms. Conn said to my interpreter, Mr. Charles, "Tell Iris to move over next to Nina so she can catch her up." She usually talked around me like that. Mr. Charles had told her so many times that she could just talk *to* me, and he would interpret the message instead of always saying "Tell Iris . . ." Finally he gave up reminding her. She was never going to get it.

Also, I didn't need help catching up, and I for sure didn't want it from Nina.

"I'll catch myself up," I signed. When Mr. Charles voiced that for Ms. Conn, her face turned even meaner than usual, which I hadn't thought was possible. She didn't say anything else—just jerked a pointed finger to the space next to Nina's desk.

The plan made sense to Ms. Conn because she thought Nina was the smartest person in class, and Nina thought she knew sign language. She'd checked out a library book about it, so that made her an expert. Some people have the kind of confidence that lets them get away with being clueless.

Nina signed something to me as I slid my desk over to her territory.

I asked Mr. Charles, *"Did she just call herself a giant squirrel?"*

He clamped his lips together and looked away while answering, *"I think she meant 'great partner.' "*

That was what I'd figured, but trying to make Mr. Charles laugh was one of my favorite things.

I leaned over to the next row to look at Clarissa Gold's book. Mr. Charles interpreted my question when I asked Clarissa what we were working on. Nina tried to barge in with her flapping hands and made-up sign language. When I ignored her she got dangerously close to my face. As if I couldn't see her. My eyes stayed on Mr. Charles, since he actually did know what he was doing. Nina's hands were like a swarm of flies I wanted to swat away, so it felt good to flick the wrist of an open hand to sign *"Stop it"* to her. After Mr. Charles interpreted that, he added that it might be distracting to have two people signing at the same time. Usually he didn't jump in like that because he wanted me to take care of things for myself, so Nina must have been annoying him, too.

After a few minutes Ms. Conn came by to ask Nina, "Are you doing okay, helping Iris?"

"Yes, I think she's catching on," she answered.

Catching on. I looked back down at my work so I wouldn't turn into one of those cartoon characters with steam shooting out of their ears. After I scribbled down the last answer in the workbook, I slammed it closed and signed, *"Finished."*

I was about to take out my phone so I could read the new issue of *Antique Radio Magazine* I'd downloaded that morning. If I opened a book on my desk, I could probably read some of the magazine by looking down at the phone on my lap.

While my hand was sliding into my backpack, Ms. Conn said something to me and pointed at her mouth. She'd tried that before, as if that would magically help me understand her. One night at dinner I told my parents, *"Hey, I'm not Deaf anymore. Ms. Conn pointed to her lips while she talked, and everything was perfectly clear. Can't believe you didn't think of it."*

On the first day of school, Ms. Conn tried to hold Mr. Charles's hands still to force me to read her lips instead of watching his signing. I didn't catch what Mr. Charles said to her, but she let go of his hands like she'd touched a hot stove, and didn't try that ever again.

We ignored the lip pointing, and Mr. Charles interpreted what Ms. Conn said: I'd have to redo my poetry assignment from last week. That didn't make sense. The poem I'd turned in was really good.

When Ms. Conn returned with my paper, she looked like she'd just bitten into a sour pickle. A normal expression for her, but right then, it looked like she was smelling something really bad at the same time she was biting that pickle.

The red ink was the first thing I noticed when Ms. Conn handed back my paper. In the margin were the words *This does not rhyme!*

Which wasn't true. The poem came from a sign language storytelling game I used to do with Grandpa. One of us would start a story, and we'd take turns adding to it, one sign at a time. The trick was our hands had to keep the same shape for the whole story. Like if we started out with a closed fist, every sign for the rest of the story had to be made with a fist too. We'd go on and on like that until one of us couldn't think of something to add without breaking the handshape rule.

My favorite story started with a tree, full with leaves. A leaf blew away with a gust of wind, then landed in a river, floated down a stream, and onto the bank. It ended with a bird swooping in to grab the leaf to add to her nest in another tree. We told that story with our hands open like the number five the whole way through.

It didn't look the same on paper. Paper is flat, so I couldn't use all the space above and below and around it that I needed to tell the story right. And the words in English don't have the same shapes as they do in sign language. But here's how it looked when I wrote it down:

Leaves waving
Blowing, twirling
Floating current
Land on a riverbank
Mother bird grabs the leaf
And builds a new nest.

Sure, it didn't rhyme the way English words do, but I thought maybe it would be okay to turn in if I explained all that. At the top of the paper I'd written a note about the poem. I wondered if Ms. Conn had even read that part.

A red line crossed through the poem, ruining it. I took out my own red pen and glared at Ms. Conn. Below her *This does not rhyme!* message, I wrote *It does to me.*

Ever since Grandpa died, I'd wondered if he could still see me, if he was with me in some way. Right then, I hoped more than anything that he was nowhere near me. I didn't want him to see what Ms. Conn had done to our story. To us.

Everyone turned and looked at me as I crumpled the paper into a ball. Nina held a finger to her lips as always, like it was her job to remind me that things made noise and that I wasn't supposed to do any of them. But I did not throw the paper at her face. I flung it across the room, where it landed in the trash can, followed by the tree and the leaves and the river and the bird with her new nest, all slashed to pieces by a red line.

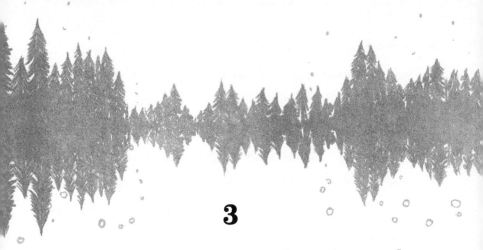

3

Even though electronics is a science-y thing, science was the one class where I wasn't reading about it on the sly. Usually I paid attention to what was going on in there because I liked science and my teacher, Sofia Alamilla. I even liked the way her name rolled off my hand like a wave when I spelled it out.

Ms. Alamilla wrote the letters *Hz* on the board. "Remember what this stands for?" she asked.

A few hands went up, and Ms. Alamilla called on me. I spelled out *"h-e-r-t-z,"* and Mr. Charles voiced "hertz" for her and the class.

"That's right," said Ms. Alamilla. "And what does it measure?"

"The frequency of sound."

I wondered why Ms. Alamilla was reviewing frequencies. We'd taken the test on it months ago.

"I found something that ties in nicely with what

we're studying now," she said, as if she'd heard me. "It's about a special whale, and you'll see why the frequency of his song is important."

Ms. Alamilla pressed some keys on the computer at her desk, and her eyeglasses reflected the video that played. The projector screen in front of the room showed a big blue square with "No Signal" in one corner.

I was heading to Ms. Alamilla's desk even before she signed *"Please help"* to me. After restarting the video and pausing it, I connected the computer to the projector's signal, then clicked the "CC" at the bottom of the screen to turn on the closed-captioning.

The video started out with a whale swimming in the ocean. Because of the captions, I could read the words on the screen instead of from Mr. Charles's hands. The dark gray-blue body of the whale filled up the screen, his tail waving up and down.

The narrator in the video talked about a whale called Blue 55, who swam around by himself and not in a pod like most whales. As far as anyone knew, it had always been that way; he didn't have any friends or a family to swim with or talk to. He was a type of baleen whale— the kind that ate plankton and small fish, not the kind with teeth that ate squid and seals. But he was a hybrid. His mother was a blue whale, and his father was a fin whale.

"The problem," said the narrator, "is Blue 55's unique voice. Most whales call out at frequencies of thirty-five hertz and lower, while this lonely whale's sounds are at around fifty-five hertz."

Only about twenty hertz off, but it made a big difference. He was speaking a language that only he knew.

"Furthermore, his song is in a unique pattern; even if other whales can hear him, they don't understand what he's saying. Blue 55 likely couldn't communicate with his own parents."

My stomach tightened into a ball. I wanted another whale on the screen to swim up to Blue 55, or at least look at him.

"The strange calls of Blue 55 were first detected by naval sonar in the late 1980s. Marine biologists figured out what was making the sounds and why the whale was all alone in the ocean."

I didn't notice until the words on the screen blurred that my eyes were watery. Mr. Charles handed me a tissue from his pocket. Maybe I'd sniffled or something.

"Allergies," I signed without looking away from the video.

The narrator went on to say that researchers from a marine sanctuary had tried to put a tracker on Blue 55 the year before so they could follow his migration pattern, which was also weird and unlike other whales'. They did get a sample of his skin to test. That was how they figured out his parents had been different species. Before they could attach the tracker to him, he dove down and swam away. He wouldn't need to resurface for a breath for another twenty minutes. Without a tracker on him, the only way anyone ever knew where he was swimming was from underwater microphones that picked up his song.

I didn't remember standing up, but when the video ended and Ms. Alamilla started talking, I had to look down to see Mr. Charles. Everyone's eyes were on me as I slid back down into my chair. My textbook was on the floor—I must have knocked it off my desk when I stood up. I left it at my feet.

"Can you imagine that?" Ms. Alamilla asked. "Swimming around for all those years, unable to communicate with anyone?"

Yes.

She said something else about frequencies, but I

wasn't paying attention anymore. I looked through Mr. Charles, as if I could still see that whale on the screen.

Blue 55 didn't have a pod of friends or a family who spoke his language. But he still sang. He was calling and calling, and no one heard him.

4

He hadn't always swum alone. Long ago, when the loudest sounds in the ocean were the songs of whales, he'd had a pod.

Those first whales had tried to talk to him. Every day they worked to change their songs to something like his.

He returned their calls, but his sounds meant nothing to them.

He heard the other whales. But nothing he sang back made sense. They thought he didn't understand.

They communicated to one another past him, through him, across him. Like he was a coral reef or a kelp forest they passed by. But he heard all of it.

He understood them when they despaired, giving up on ever hearing him, and when they lamented he would never be able to contribute to the pod. He couldn't warn them of a coming predator or announce the scent of waters that were good for feeding.

Yes, I can, he bellowed. *There, waves full of krill.* He turned to show them the way. He sang his message, struggling to match the sounds of the whales around him. But the sea grabbed his song and dragged it away, too high for the others to reach.

One night, when he awoke to float to the surface for a breath, he found himself alone. After so much time, with so many songs unheard, his family had left him.

He called out *Where are you?* and *What will I do now?* knowing no answer would come, knowing the sounds held meaning only for himself.

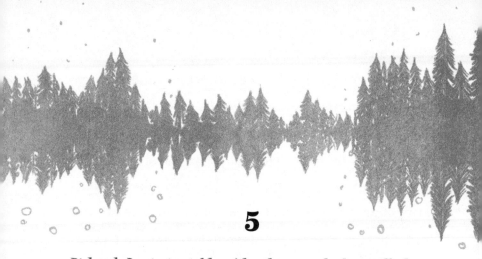

5

At lunch I sat at a table with other people, but still alone. I could actually read lips all right—not that I'd ever tell Ms. Conn. No matter how good I was, there'd be no way to catch everything. Too many sounds look the same, and in a group of people, it's impossible to pick up more than a word or two here and there. It's even worse if they're eating. Some kids tried to remember to look at me when they talked. Then they'd get into a conversation with everyone else, too fast for me to keep up. A couple of the kids knew the sign language alphabet and would spell out sentences letter by letter. That took forever, so I'd tell them to just go ahead and write it. Whenever I spelled something back, they didn't catch it anyway, unless I slowed down so much that by the time I got to the end of the sentence, they'd forgotten the beginning.

Some people at my table were in my science class.

I was still thinking about the whale called Blue 55, and wondered if they were too. It didn't look like anyone was talking about him. I wanted to ask if they thought he liked swimming around by himself or if he wanted friends. Maybe he'd tried singing like the other whales and couldn't do it, or he was happy singing his own song.

Nina walked by with some of her friends and waved like she wanted to tell me something super important. Even when I understood her, she never said anything important. But she had seen the Blue 55 video, and obviously she was interested in sign language. I took a deep breath and decided to give it a try.

As clearly as possible I signed to her, *"What did you think of that whale?"*

Nina pointed at my lunch and signed something that made absolutely no sense. I couldn't even figure out what she was trying to get at.

Maybe the message was jumbled because she was excited and signing too fast, as if her hands couldn't keep up with her brain.

I held up a hand to try to slow her down. Numbers and letters were easy enough to understand, so I shook a letter B to sign *"Blue,"* then tapped the air twice with a five handshape. *Blue 55.* I shrugged a little and raised my eyebrows with a question. It should've been perfectly clear I was asking, "So, what did you think of that whale?"

Somehow, she still didn't seem to get it, and I didn't understand whatever she was trying to say. Nothing that looked like *"whale"* or *"ocean"* or *"song."*

I gave up and turned to Sanjay, who was sitting across from me and talking about a new level he'd unlocked in a video game or something like that. Out of the corner of my eye, I saw Nina signing even more furiously. Her friends backed away to avoid getting smacked in the face by her flailing arms. Even though she was the one making a scene, I was getting the attention. Sanjay pointed to tell me I should be looking at Nina, but I waved him off, as if I were dying to know the rest of his video game story. I took a quick glance to see if Nina had given up yet. My face burned as she moved in closer. Great. This girl couldn't recognize a hint if it ran up and set her hands on fire. I reached into my backpack and ripped a piece of paper from a notebook.

"What's everyone doing this weekend?" was the first thing I thought of to start a new conversation. Nina was right next to me. I knew this not from looking at her, but from the breeze created by her hands waving at the side of my head. Finally I turned to look, because

everyone was pointing by then. What I witnessed was amazing. Not even one sign made sense. I signed to Nina, *"I don't understand you,"* then turned back to the group. Still she didn't give up. She leaned over, forcing me to see her, and signed with her hands right in my face. I couldn't take it anymore. My face burned hotter. Everyone looked at me like I was the dumb one for not understanding.

I pushed her away and signed, *"Leave me alone!"* I didn't mean to push her so hard, but she ended up crashing into the people at the next table and landing on the floor. Nina's mouth was open wide, as if she were yelling. She must have been making a lot of noise since people from all the way across the cafeteria stood up for a better view. The lunch duty teachers made their way to our table then, their faces full of concern. One of their mouths formed the words "What happened?"

A teacher helped Nina up. She rubbed her elbow where she'd landed but seemed fine otherwise. I stood up and swung my backpack over my shoulder. Even though the bell hadn't rung, I headed to the principal's office. That was where they were going to send me anyway.

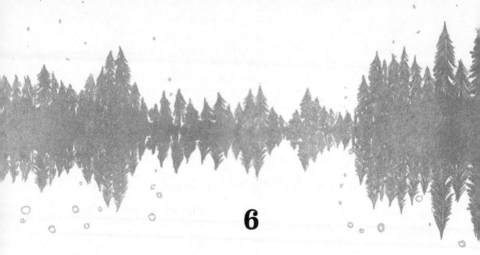

6

The secretary was picking up the phone when she saw me coming, and I waved to her on my way into Principal Shelton's office. Ms. Shelton wasn't there, so I went ahead and rearranged the furniture. I slid the black chair over to one side of the desk. Mr. Charles would sit there, so I could see both him and Ms. Shelton at the same time. I sank into my favorite chair and stared at the ceiling while I waited.

Ms. Shelton came in and sat behind her desk, then held out her arms, as if she were saying, "Well?"

I shrugged. No point in chatting until Mr. Charles got there. I reached up to the pendant I wore around my neck, the one made from an old Zenith radio knob. They used to emboss the wooden knobs with a raised Z-shape lightning bolt. In my room at home, I had a collection of antique radios. I did some repair work for Mr. Gunnar's antique shop, and sometimes—okay, a lot of times—I ended up buying radios from him after I fixed them. I'd made the pendant so I'd have a piece of my collection with me even when I was away from home. While we waited I traced the jagged edges of the letter with my fingertip.

Mr. Charles came in a few minutes later. *"Welcome,"* I signed as he took the seat across from me.

I pointed to a picture on Ms. Shelton's desk that I hadn't seen before. *"New grandbaby?"*

"Yes, that's Henry," she said after Mr. Charles interpreted my question. "Now, tell me what happened in the cafeteria."

Ms. Shelton knew what happened; I was sure of that. She always wanted to get my side of the story. One of those things they teach in principal school—find out what happened, then question the kid to see if they lie about it. Mr. Charles interpreted between Ms. Shelton and me as I filled her in.

"Nina was only trying to ask what you were having for lunch," she said.

I actually slapped myself in the forehead. All this because Nina wanted to know what kind of sandwich I had?

"She was trying to make conversation with you, Iris. To be friendly."

"No she's not," I signed. *"She's trying to show off and pretend she knows something she doesn't. She needs to keep her hands out of my face."*

Ms. Shelton reminded me of the school's zero tolerance policy for fighting. I tried to argue that I was only removing someone's hands from my personal space, but it was no use. At school that counted as fighting.

"This isn't fair." I slumped back in the chair and looked out the window at the parking lot.

Mr. Charles waved to get my attention and interpreted the rest of what Ms. Shelton said.

"The other students at the lunch table did say that you tried to get Nina to stop when she got so close to you. We'll talk to her about respecting personal space. If it happens again, tell a teacher instead of shoving someone."

"Okay." I left it at that. Ms. Shelton probably wouldn't like it if I pointed out that shoving was a lot quicker than flagging down a teacher and scribbling a note to explain what was going on.

I'd have in-school suspension for the next two days, starting right then. That meant I'd sit in one room all day, and my teachers would send my work there. Fine with me. Regular suspension would've been even better. At home I could fly through my schoolwork and then start on some radio repairs. That was probably why they didn't do it—because they'd figured out it was too much like a vacation.

Then Ms. Shelton slipped in the worst part. "And you'll have to apologize to Nina when you return to class."

Maybe she'd forget about that.

By the end of school day, I had a text from Mom. *Get straight home after school.* Of course Ms. Shelton had called to let her know of my sentencing. I biked toward home after school, but I wasn't in a big hurry to get there. My parents had told me I'd be in Serious Trouble if I got sent to the principal's office again, even though there was a whole month left of school. I wasn't sure what they meant by "Serious Trouble," but some things were better left a mystery.

That morning I'd been working on a radio repair for Mr. Gunnar, a mint-colored Zenith from the 1950s. That was why I was a little late getting to school. I was so close to fixing it, but then I realized I didn't have what I needed to finish the job. Mr. Gunnar wasn't in a hurry—he always told me to take the time I needed to do the job right. But I couldn't stand to leave anything sitting around broken. It chased me until I couldn't ignore it anymore.

The junkyard was on the way home. Sort of.

At the gate of Moe's Junk Emporium, I hopped off my bike even before it stopped rolling. My eyes scanned the dead appliances section as I ran up the sidewalk. Always so many dishwashers and washing machines. But there ... There was a monster-size TV/radio/record player set. Not that it had a big screen; I mean, it was thick. You'd have to set it at least three feet away from the wall.

I ran over for a closer look. Made by Admiral; in the 1950s, I was pretty sure. The set featured decades of dust that had sunk into the scratches of the wood cabinet, and tatters of cloth hanging from the speaker. Hopefully the insides were in better shape. The TV and record player weren't much use, but the radio might have the exact parts I needed.

I took out my phone to text Grandpa. It was the kind of thing he'd pick up for me before someone else grabbed it. I typed a few words before I caught myself. Sometimes I'd think of something to tell him, before remembering he wasn't there to answer me. Then I felt bad for forgetting. Shouldn't I always feel it? Missing him?

After erasing the message I changed it to *Wish you were still here.* Even though he wouldn't receive it, I clicked send before slipping the phone back into my pocket. He seemed closer then, like just sending that short message would somehow let him know I was thinking of him. *I haven't forgotten you. Sometimes I just don't remember you're not here.*

My brother, Tristan, could drive me back later to get the set, but it might be gone by then. If I asked Mom or Dad to pick it up, they'd wonder why I was at Moe's instead of at home.

I'd ask Moe to hold it for me. He knew me well enough by now, so it'd take just a minute to tell him I was interested in the set. But when I ran into the trailer that served as the office, Moe wasn't behind the desk smoking a cigar like he always was. Some guy a little older than Tristan sat there, watching a TV show where people threw chairs at one another. The patch on his blue work shirt read "Jimmy Joe."

Jimmy Joe stood up and said something when he noticed me in the doorway. I never liked talking to people I didn't know. This was an emergency, so I would. But by "talk," I mean "write notes back and forth." I hated the way people looked at me when they didn't understand my Deaf accent. Since I didn't know if I talked very well, I'd rather not do it. Plus, I never liked the way my voice felt. As much as I loved feeling sound from a radio speaker, vibrations in my throat annoyed me, as if they didn't belong there. Kind of like how I loved electronics, but not on my own ears.

At the desk I scribbled on a notepad: *Can you save that Admiral set out there for me? I'll come back for it later.*

He looked back at me after reading the note, and his face was a question. I pointed to my ear and then shook my head to let him know that these ears were as busted as everything else around there.

His eyes widened like they did with most people. A second of panic like they're not sure what to do with me or like I might explode in front of them.

"Can you, uh, read lips? Or talk?" he asked, pointing back and forth from his mouth to mine.

Maybe, I thought, *but how about just reading that note in your hand?* I tapped the paper he was holding.

He recovered, then pointed out the window. "It don't work." His mouth was really wide when he formed the words. He was probably yelling. He shook his head and waved his hands to emphasize the point.

I held back an eye roll. Of course it didn't work. Even if it worked, it wouldn't really work. Those old antenna TVs haven't been able to get a signal for years.

After taking back the note I wrote, *For parts.*

When he read that, his eyebrows rose from scared to impressed.

I'll ask my dad, Jimmy Joe wrote back. *Doctor appoint-ment. He'll be back soon.*

So Moe was his dad. From what I'd witnessed dur-ing my time as a junkyard customer, Moe started each day with a can of Budweiser and a Whole Hog break-fast sandwich from The Cattle Prod, in addition to the cigar, so a doctor visit was probably a good idea. Too bad he didn't pick a more convenient day to start caring about his health.

I added, *Tell him it's for Iris. Thanks!* While Jimmy Joe read that, I tore another page from the pad, wrote my name on it, then ripped a piece of tape from the dispenser on the desk. Without waiting for a response, I ran outside and slapped the Iris Bailey note on the Admiral. It was almost mine. Even though I was in Serious Trouble, I smiled the whole way home.

7

Tristan wasn't home yet when I got back there, but more importantly, neither was Mom. I'd have a chance to work on my radios before she came in to lecture me.

I ran upstairs to my room, where my radio collection filled shelves across three walls. I'd have to add a new shelf soon. Tools and electronics parts and wires covered the workbench I'd made out of an old door. My mom said it looked like a robot factory exploded in my room, but I knew where to find everything.

Most people were surprised when they found out I fixed old radios, but that was because most people don't notice that sound moves. If it's strong enough, it can move anything. Its waves can break glass or shake the ground or deafen a whale.

Even if they're not strong, sound waves tremble radios, too. That was why I didn't need to hear one to know if it was working. With my hand on the speaker, the vibrations let me know if a radio was playing music or crackling with static or sitting there like a box of rocks.

For me, listening to the radios was never the point. Each one of those sitting on my shelves was a reminder of something I'd done right. They weren't working until I got my hands into them. Whenever I fixed something, I felt like I'd won a contest.

I sat down next to my bed and touched the side of the Philco 38-690 cabinet radio like I did every day when I got home and every morning before I left. Of all the antique radios in my collection, this was my favorite. Since it was almost four feet tall, it sat on the floor instead of on a shelf like the others. It was from the 1930s and, in my professional opinion, the best radio ever made. Only three thousand ever existed.

For a long time I'd only seen the 38-690 in pictures. Then one day there it was, behind the counter at Mr. Gunnar's antique shop. My eyes almost fell out of my head when Mr. Gunnar said he was going to throw it away. Sure, it was in rough shape. Really rough. But I couldn't let him get rid of it. I asked if I could take it as payment for a repair I'd brought him. He said that wouldn't be fair, so he paid me *and* gave me the radio. Then I sort of felt like I was stealing from an old man.

Even though he might change his mind, I told Mr. Gunnar what the Philco could be worth if I restored it. Maybe he didn't know what he had.

A cloud of dust flew up when he patted the radio's scratched wooden cabinet. "If you do all the work this thing is going to need, you deserve to keep it."

For the next five months, I worked to bring the Philco back from the dead. When I finally finished, static hummed against my palms. With the smallest turn of the dial, the smooth rhythm of music flowed from the speaker, vibrating the whole cabinet of the radio. If anyone had asked why I was sitting there crying with my arms around a radio, I wouldn't have known how to explain it. I couldn't stop thinking about how many years it had sat quietly collecting dust and how close it had come to being thrown in the garbage because no one thought it was worth listening to.

Usually I left it on overnight, even though that would wear it out faster. While I was in bed, I could reach over and feel the vibrations against my hand and fall asleep wondering who was singing and who was listening.

The floor shook a little, announcing Mom coming up the stairs. I sat there, waiting to find out what my punishment would be. Probably I wouldn't be allowed to use my phone or visit my friend Wendell for a while.

When the door opened I turned to her and signed, *"I know, Serious Trouble. But—"*

She pointed around my room before I could explain that what had happened at school wasn't my fault. *"All of this,"* she signed, *"is out of here."*

"What?"

"Get some sheets and towels and wrap them up if you want, but as soon as Tristan gets home, you're going to help us carry everything out to the garage."

I gripped the edge of the Philco, as if I could keep it from leaving my side. *"No, that isn't fair!"*

"You said you'd stay out of trouble. We warned you about this."

"I didn't know you meant I'd lose my radios." I waved my arms at my collection. *"I didn't know you'd take everything I have."*

"You're being dramatic. It isn't everything you have. Anyway," she added before I could interrupt her, *"we have to do something to get your attention. Maybe you'll take us seriously when we say you have to learn to get along with people and follow the rules. That girl's parents are really upset with the school."*

"It's not the school's fault. Or my fault. They should be mad at themselves for raising an annoying daughter."

"It can't always be someone else's fault. If people annoy you, you have to figure out a better way to deal with it."

"Easy for you to say. There isn't a better way when everyone ignores you." Warm tears dampened my fingertips when my signing hands touched my face. I wiped my hands on my jeans. Just then, I remembered the Admiral set. I couldn't believe I'd forgotten about it. Mom's announcement about taking my radios must have short-circuited my brain.

"I have to pick up a TV from the junkyard." Hopefully she wouldn't ask when I'd been at Moe's, but I had to risk it.

"No, we're not going out to get you a new thing to add to the exact collection you're grounded from. You have enough junk anyway."

It didn't matter that I had a lot of junk. I didn't have that particular item. I tried to explain it, but Mom turned to leave. The conversation was over.

Before she walked out I waved my hand to get her attention. *"When can I have my stuff back?"*

"A little at a time, starting Monday."

"What will I do all weekend?"

"You can visit Wendell, and we'll go to Grandma's on

Saturday. You're not grounded from everything, just your electronics."

Which was everything.

When Tristan got home he told me I didn't have to help carry my things out. He knew how much it would hurt. *"Mom and I will take care of it."*

I shook my head as I slid one of my smaller radios into a pillowcase. *"That's okay. But thanks."* I really didn't want to do it, but I also didn't want to miss out on one more chance to hold my radios before they were put away.

After we hauled my stuff to the garage, I went back up to my room, which wasn't really my room anymore. The shelves were bare. So was the worktable, which just a few hours earlier had been piled with electronics parts. A thin layer of dust outlined all that was missing. An imprint in the carpet next to my bed marked where the Philco should have been.

I lay down in bed and turned toward the wall so I wouldn't have to face the emptiness.

Tristan came in later to check on me. I turned when he sat at the edge of the bed and touched my shoulder.

"You okay?" he signed.

I rolled onto my back. *"No. I will never be okay."*

"I'm sorry."

"It isn't fair. I need my stuff. It's work anyway, like for Mr. Gunnar. So they're grounding me from work, which is stupid."

"Yeah, I told Mom that. I think they want you to hang out with people instead of radios so much."

"I do hang out with people." Tristan didn't respond to that. Maybe he didn't believe me. He was always doing things with friends.

"It's just for a couple days."

"But there's this radio I really need. Mom won't let me pick it up, even if I promise not to work on it yet."

"Where is it?"

"Moe's." I sat up. "Will you go get it for me? Please? It looks heavy since it's in a cabinet with a TV and record player, but you're strong enough to load it into your truck."

He said what looked like "Ummm ..." and ran a hand through his hair. Unlike me, he could do that without getting his hand stuck. He had Dad's smooth light brown hair, instead of thick dark curls like Mom and me. All I got from Dad was pale skin that turned pink and more freckled in the sun, instead of Mom's, which tanned.

"Please," I signed again. "Do you know how many vacuum tubes are in there?"

"No idea. How many?"

"I don't know. More than I need. I was going to look it up. Plus tube sockets, wires, transformers, caps . . ."

Tristan laughed and threw his hands up in surrender, which, as it happens, looks like the sign for "give up." "Okay, okay. But then what? You don't think Mom and Dad will notice?"

"Hide it in the garage with everything else. Then we'll bring it up to my closet when they're not here."

"Okay, hold on. Be right back." He signed "hold" like he was clutching something in his fist and not by pointing an index finger up like people do all the time, as if they were saying Wait a minute and then never getting back to you. Tristan knew I hated that.

After a few minutes Tristan came back and waved me to the doorway. "Let's go."

"Me? Go where?"

"I just chugged the last of the milk and then told Mom I'd go out to pick up more."

I jumped up and slid into my shoes. Milk wasn't the only thing we'd be picking up.

Moe was back at his usual place behind the desk in the junkyard's office trailer.

"How was the doctor appointment?" I asked.

Tristan voiced my question, and Moe answered, "I'm healthy as a horse."

Not any horse I'd want to ride, but I wasn't going to mention that. *"How much for the Admiral set?"*

Even though Tristan was there, Moe communicated with me like he always did and held up two fingers on one hand and five on the other.

I pretended to consider the twenty-five-dollar offer, as if I wasn't desperate enough to pay whatever he asked. Before we left home I'd grabbed two twenties from my repair money envelope.

I held up two fingers on one hand and formed the other into an *O* handshape.

Moe nodded and gave me a thumbs-up, then followed us outside after I handed him a twenty. He helped Tristan lift up the set and load it into the truck. Before hopping into the passenger seat, I shook Moe's hand and hugged Tristan. I'd have to force myself to stop smiling when we got home so Mom wouldn't wonder why I was so happy.

We were pulling into the driveway when I tapped Tristan on the shoulder and signed, *"Milk!"* The reason for the trip, as far as Mom knew. He backed out and hurried to the gas station.

"Want anything?" he asked when we were inside.

"I'm almost out of gummy worms," I answered.

He squeezed my shoulder and signed, *"Pick out whatever you want."*

The hard part was when we got home. Tristan always parked in the driveway, since our two-car garage had room for only one car and a bunch of stuff. We slid the TV onto a flattened cardboard box and shoved it into the garage, stopping a couple times along the way to give my arms a rest. Finally we got it safely in the corner and covered it with garage junk. Tomorrow it would be in my closet where it belonged, and my room wouldn't feel so empty anymore.

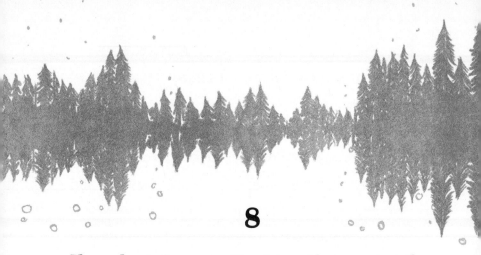

8

The weekend of my grounding dragged by even worse than I'd expected. My friend Wendell was out of town with his family, so I couldn't hang out at his house. Tristan and his friend Adam had moved the TV/radio/record player to my closet. Now and then I'd open the door to take a peek, but I couldn't crack it open yet. After clearing out my room, I didn't even have a screwdriver left. Still, I felt better just knowing the Admiral set was close by, waiting for me.

＊ While lying on my bed with my phone, I searched online for the whale. Ever since Ms. Alamilla had showed us that video in class, I'd been thinking about Blue 55 and the people who tried to tag him with the tracker.

I couldn't remember the name of the sanctuary from the video, but it came up after a quick search about Blue 55's tagging.

The "Meet Our Residents" page on the sanctuary's website showed a picture of each animal that lived there, along with a description. Either the sanctuary staff had found them injured or sick, or someone had called for help when they found them hurt in the water or on the beach. The animals lived either in large sea pens or indoor pools until they were healthy enough to return to the wild. Most of the animals were birds or seals and sea lions. One dolphin they'd have to move indoors if they couldn't release him before winter hit Alaska.

For some, the sanctuary would always be their home. The eagle who was blind in one eye couldn't hunt for food in the wild. He probably didn't understand why he couldn't fly outdoors anymore. The otter orphans had an indoor-outdoor pool to swim in. They'd have to live at the sanctuary forever too. They had lost their mothers when they were so young that they hadn't learned how to be otters. I wondered about the animals who'd been taken in when they were older and still remembered their old homes. The sanctuary staff would release them close to where they'd been found, in hopes they'd find their families. They couldn't promise it would happen, though. The released animals might have to make it on their own.

At the top of a page labeled "The Staff" was a picture of a few people in light blue shirts with their arms around one another, smiling in front of the sanctuary. The caption of the photo said that it was the expedition team that tried to tag Blue 55 the year before.

After scrolling through some of the posts, I found one about the failed attempt to tag Blue 55. The tracker they wanted to put on him would collect information not just about where he swam, but other things too, like his heart rate. It would also record his song. They'd share information about him on their website if they ever did tag him. Now I really wished they'd tagged him. If they shared what they recorded from that, I'd get to feel his song and heartbeat through a computer speaker.

A picture showed Blue 55's back arching out of the water, next to a small boat. Mounted to the front of the boat was a metal platform with railings on either side. A woman wearing a stocking cap and a green fleece jacket stood at the edge of the platform, holding a long metal pole outstretched toward the whale. It looked like she'd topple over the railing and into the ocean if she leaned over any farther to reach him. The caption read: "Near miss: Blue 55 takes a dive before sanctuary staffer Andi Rivera can attach a tracking device."

The tracker at the end of the pole looked close

enough to brush the whale's back. A grimace lined Andi's face, either from effort or disappointment. The next photo showed water cascading down Blue 55's huge tail as he started his deep dive. Andi had been so close to him before he slipped away. Maybe she was only interested in him as a scientist, but she tried so hard to reach him; maybe she really cared about him, too.

If Blue 55 followed the route he usually did, he'd be near the sanctuary soon. A new post said that the team would try again to tag him. They didn't say what they would do differently next time, so they could get close enough to attach the tracker before he swam away. Maybe there was a way to get him to stick around a little longer.

At the bottom of the page was a link to more information about Blue 55's communication. That article used piano keys to describe whale song frequencies. If you sit down at a piano and hit the lowest key, the very first one on the left, that plays the frequency of 27.5 hertz. That's the frequency of most baleen whale songs. They sing lower than that, too—like twenty hertz or ten hertz—but pianos didn't have a key that played that low. Count over to key number thirteen, and you'll play fifty-five hertz—Blue 55's frequency, and the reason he couldn't talk to any other whale.

Already I was thinking of a way to reach out to him. At my desk I grabbed a scrap of paper to jot down some notes. I didn't know yet how it would work, but maybe the people who wanted to tag Blue 55 could find a way to sing back to him and hold his attention with something that sounded a bit like himself.

As I wrote, a thought came up that crumbled the edges of my plan. Maybe he was like that sei whale on the beach, except that he'd found a way to survive.

On the sanctuary's post about Blue 55's communication, I scanned the comments section to see if anyone wondered the same thing I had. No one suggested it yet, so I scrolled back up and left a comment.

Maybe the whale is deaf.

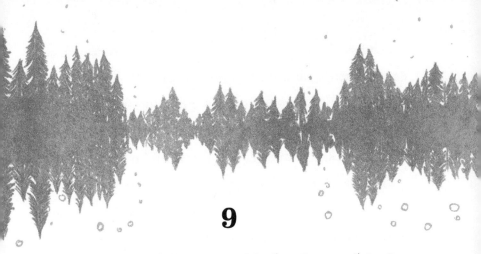

9

On the way to Oak Manor to visit Grandma on Saturday, Tristan touched my shoulder and signed, *"Hungry?"* He smiled like something was funny.

Actually, I was starving. *"Yeah, why?"*

"Your stomach is rumbling like an airplane engine."

I covered my stomach with my hands to muffle the sound and smiled back at him. *"I doubt that. An airplane engine is over one hundred decibels."* However loud a stomach rumble was, it had to be a lot less than that.

That morning I'd been too nervous to eat breakfast. Normally I was excited to visit Grandma. Other than Wendell, she was the only Deaf person I got to talk to anymore.

Lately it was like I needed a bridge to get to her. One of us would say something; then the conversation would fizzle out, and we were back to sitting there trying to come up with something else to say. It used to be that when I got together with my grandparents, we'd sign nonstop, catching up on everything in our lives and laughing at our own jokes and stories that made sense only in sign language. Maybe Grandpa had been our bridge, and we didn't notice it until he was gone.

Grandma had moved to Oak Manor just a few weeks earlier. Before that she still lived in the house she'd shared with Grandpa for forever. One day, about a month after Grandpa died, she didn't answer the door when we went to visit her. She didn't reply to text messages either. Her car wasn't in the garage.

We let ourselves in with the spare key that Mom had, then searched the house. I checked the study. On her desk was a lamp I'd made her out of an old wine bottle. I'd filled it with shells and sea glass we'd found at the beach. Next to that was a picture of Grandpa and me building a sandcastle.

Grandma, where are you? I looked up then at a framed picture on the wall and felt like she was teasing me with an answer. Below the picture of a whale swimming in the ocean was a quote from her favorite book, *Moby-Dick:* "I know not all that may be coming, but be it what it will, I'll go to it laughing."

I found Mom in Grandma's room, sitting on the bed with her phone.

"*Maybe she's at the beach,*" I suggested.

Mom shook her head. "*She never drives that far. I'm checking with her friends to see if they know anything. I'm sure she's fine.*" Before she pulled me in for a hug, I caught the expression on her face. It matched the worry I felt.

Dad finally called the police.

An hour later the police called back. They found Grandma more than one hundred miles away at the Gulf Coast, walking the stretch of beach where we used to live.

After she got back home, she tried to explain that she'd left because she was like Ishmael in *Moby-Dick*. Sometimes she had too much of a drizzly November in her soul and had to get to the sea. She used to travel with Grandpa all the time, she said, and everyone should stop making such a big deal over it.

"*Why didn't you at least tell us where you were going?*" Mom asked her.

"*Because you would've talked me out of it.*" No one argued with that.

Mom finally convinced her to move to Oak Manor, which was an apartment complex for old people. Grandma said the house was too big for one person to take care of anyway, so she'd go. I didn't believe her.

She looked like she just didn't feel strong enough to keep fighting. Sometimes that was the easier choice.

My parents promised to take her to the beach in the summer, maybe, when they weren't so busy with work.

Sometimes I worried that Grandma wouldn't make it until summer. Her November had gone on for three months already, and it seemed like she might be stuck there wandering and shivering forever. So there was something I couldn't fix.

Before we went through the sliding glass doors at Oak Manor, Mom gave me a tight hug that lasted a few seconds longer than most. Then she stepped back and smoothed my hair and signed, *"I love you."* She did that every time we visited Grandma. Just to me, never to Tristan.

"Love you, too, Mom."

Tristan and I headed upstairs with Dad, while Mom went to the social worker's office to ask if Grandma was making friends yet.

It was almost noon when we got to Grandma's apartment, but she looked like she'd just rolled out of bed. She wore a pair of sweatpants and a gray T-shirt she'd probably slept in. After giving each of us a hug, she invited us to come in and sit down.

"Where's Mom?" she asked.

"She'll be up in a minute," I answered. "Talking to the staff downstairs."

Grandma smiled. "About your uncooperative grandmother."

"So that's where Iris gets it." Dad laughed at his own joke.

Grandma sat next to me on the couch and asked, "How's school?"

"The same," I answered.

"Sorry to hear that." She turned to my dad and signed, "Maybe Iris could transfer to Bridgewood and be around other Deaf students." She signed slowly for my dad and used her voice, too. She could hear a little, and people who knew her could mostly understand what she said. And Dad never had learned sign language very well. He could get by okay, but it wasn't like we could have a real conversation. I didn't expect him to know it as well as Mom. She had Deaf parents, so she was signing before she could talk. I just wished he put more effort into learning it. He said he'd always been more of a "numbers person" than a "words person" and that it was hard to learn a new language. Seems like having a kid you could barely talk to would be harder.

I held my breath, wondering if Dad might agree with her. Bridgewood was a district with a big deaf education program about a twenty-minute drive from our neighborhood. Deaf kids, like my friend Wendell, from three school districts went there. But Mom insisted on me going to Timber Oaks with all my "neighborhood friends." I'd pointed out to her that I didn't have any of those anyway, but it didn't help. She wanted to stick with the plan she'd come up with when we first moved to town.

Once in a while Grandma brought up my going to Bridgewood. Maybe Dad would agree with her this time, without Mom there to say I should keep going to school with the same people I'd been with all along. Dad didn't seem to care much either way. If he thought Grandma had a good idea, maybe he'd mention it to Mom later.

Dad said something while throwing in a couple of signs like *"think"* and *"ship"* and then waved his hand. From what I could piece together from the signs and what I read on his mouth, it was something like "I think that ship has sailed." He used figures of speech all the time, even though most of them didn't make sense in sign language. Usually I could figure out what he meant, like if I'd read the phrase in a book or it was one he said a lot. Once in a while an English expression was similar to one in sign language. Like if you pretend you're pulling a hair from your head, that's like the English phrase "by a hair." Usually they didn't match up so nicely.

"What do you mean?" I didn't see why he thought it was too late for me to switch school districts. Why should I stay in the same place just because I'd been there for so long?

"Nothing," Dad signed. *"It's not important."* He looked at Grandma and said, "Iris has gotten used to her school."

Heat rushed to my face. I probably looked sunburned. This was a conversation about my school, and Dad wanted to leave me out of it. Even worse than talking around me was talking *about* me like I wasn't there.

"Really?" Grandma asked. She didn't look like she was waiting for an answer. Her eyes shifted over to me.

I leaned forward and waved my arm so Dad would look at me again. *"It's important to me."*

"You know, it's like 'train gone,'" signed Tristan.

"I know that," I signed. *"I meant, why is Dad saying that about school?"*

"Train?" Dad asked.

I almost had to sit on my hands to keep from answering, *"Nothing. It's not important."*

"Remember? That's how you do that phrase in sign

language," Tristan answered. "*Instead of saying, 'That ship has sailed' or 'You missed the boat.'*"

"*I've shown you that before,*" I told Dad. "*But that's not the point.*" Why had that ship sailed? I'd be starting junior high next year anyway. Might as well hop on the next boat or train or whatever with people I could talk to.

Mom walked in then with some flyers.

"*Hi, Mom,*" she signed, and came over to the couch to give Grandma a hug.

Grandma gave her a small smile and signed, "*I know, I'm in trouble.*"

"*You're not in trouble,*" Mom said. "*But I was hoping you'd be socializing more. It isn't good for you to be by yourself all the time.*"

Tristan sat on the floor in front of the couch and took a flyer from Mom.

"*I know,*" Grandma said. "*I never feel like doing anything. I'll get out sometime.*"

"*Look.*" Tristan pointed out some events on the calendar. "*They have a lot of stuff going on. Movie nights, games, a field trip to the zoo.*"

"*Nothing's the same without Grandpa.*"

One reason my parents suggested Oak Manor to

Grandma—besides all the staff who'd help keep an eye on her—was that there was a Deaf group who did things together. She chatted with a couple of them, but that was it. Grandma and Grandpa always seemed so outgoing, so fun. All that had drained out of her now that he wasn't around anymore.

They'd met in college, where they were in a Deaf theater group together. Sometimes the plays they performed were all in sign language, and they'd have interpreters speaking the parts for "the sign language impaired." Other times they interpreted plays for the school, after rehearsing for weeks with the cast. They were so good at bringing a play to life that it wasn't just deaf people in the audience who loved watching them—everyone did. That was what they'd told me, anyway.

Mom brushed a lock of Grandma's hair back with her hand. *"You're not taking care of yourself."* She found a hairbrush in the bathroom, then sat on the other side of Grandma and motioned for her to turn toward me so she could brush her hair. Grandma's hair had been a long silvery waterfall for as long as I could remember. All the tangles in it that day made me wonder how long it had been since she'd brushed it.

I rubbed the lightning bolt Z on my necklace. There we were again, so close but with the Gulf of Mexico between us.

Maybe there was a way Grandpa could still bridge us together.

"Handshape game?" I asked.

Grandma shook her head. *"That was Grandpa's thing."*

"And now it'll be our thing." I waited, ready for her to argue back.

"Okay. What shape?"

I held up my index fingers.

Grandma nodded and motioned for me to start.

I looked up and drew the sun in the sky, squinting to show its brightness.

Grandma looked up too, then shook her head and put a finger to her lips. *"There is no sun."*

Fine, then, it'd be nighttime. I showed a star in the sky.

Grandma added, *"It's the only star."*

Why couldn't I have picked any other shape, one that wouldn't lend itself to such lonely signs? I wanted to erase everything and then open my hands to show a sky full of stars, but that would break the pattern I'd started. I'd make it work.

I looked up as if I could see it. *"No, there's a shooting star."* I drew its path zipping across the sky.

Grandma showed the shooting star traveling farther and farther away. She pointed to the first star, alone in the sky again.

My turn. Two people walked together, side by side. One of them pointed out the star, and they both looked up and smiled.

On Grandma's turn, one of those people flew up to the sky to join that star, leaving the other person all alone.

I didn't want the game to end that way, leaving that person standing on the earth all alone watching a star. But I couldn't think of what else to add to the story.

I lost.

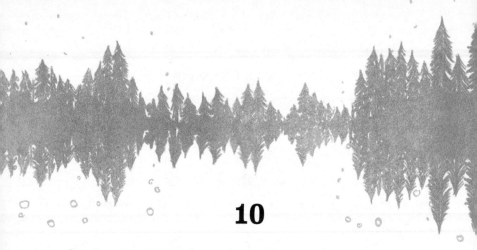

10

By the time I got home from Grandma's, a reply to my comment on the sanctuary's post was waiting for me.

Great point, Iris. We wondered about that too, but we think Blue 55 wouldn't sing at all if he were deaf. Sometimes he swims long distances to other whales, so it seems like he's following their sounds. Perhaps he has something like tone deafness, and he just can't tell he isn't singing like the others. Or for some reason he's not able to produce the same sounds.

Sometimes he's quiet for weeks at a time, and we worry that he's given up (or that he's no longer alive), but then he starts singing again. It seems he keeps trying to communicate, but there's nothing out there that understands his songs.

So he wasn't deaf; he just couldn't match the calls of the whales around him.

Before reading the rest of the message, I checked the expedition team's photos again to see who'd replied to me. The name at the top of the reply read "Andi Rivera." Andi was the woman in the photo who'd tried to tag Blue 55 the year before. The picture of the team posing together in their blue shirts showed a better view of her. Her long black hair was pulled back into a ponytail, and she looked like she was laughing. The sun, or the cold wind, had turned the cheeks of her brown face rosy.

We might never find out why whales sing, but as a scientist, I'm always thinking and looking for answers. Why Blue 55 sings when no other whale answers back is an even bigger mystery. Maybe he just likes to sing, and it doesn't matter that it's an unusual song. A lot of people think that Blue 55 is lonely. But I wonder, do we believe that because we're the ones who are lonely?

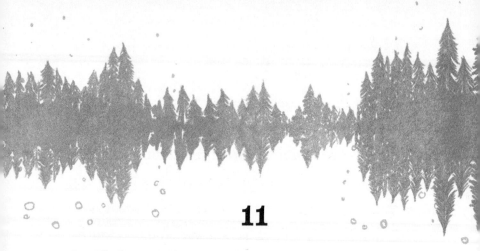

11

Ms. Shelton didn't forget about the apology thing. She told Ms. Conn I had to apologize to Nina before returning to class. Mr. Charles helped me come up with what to tell her. Even though it was Nina's fault, "Sorry you bothered me so much I had to shove you" wasn't going to work.

Mr. Charles walked with me to Nina's desk to interpret. *"Sorry I hurt you."*

She smiled a little and signed something that looked like *"pie."*

"All right," Mr. Charles corrected while biting his lip.

As soon as I got home that afternoon, I raced upstairs. Finally I'd have my radios back. Some of them, anyway. Enough to work on. For a while I stood in my bedroom doorway, looking around at the few items that were back on the shelves where they belonged.

First I had to put my workshop back in order. Mom had returned the tools and parts but didn't know where anything belonged. The Admiral set was too heavy for me to drag into my room, so I sat on the closet floor with my screwdriver. After I opened the back panel, I sat there for a minute and stared at the dust-covered parts. The work would go faster if I didn't have my thick leather gloves on, but I told my parents I'd always wear them. Unplugged or not, the radios I worked on weren't as safe as new models. Back when that old stuff was made, it was your own dumb fault if you died of electrocution.

At first glance I could tell that at least a couple of the vacuum tubes weren't any good. No obvious cracks, but the cloudy white coating inside the glass tubes let me know it was time to toss them. They'd look pretty on a Christmas tree, but I'd throw them into the recycling bin. Mom had told me enough already with the busted vacuum tube–ornaments.

Even so, that old set turned out to be worth all the trouble. When I finished the cleaning and testing of the tubes, I had five good ones.

No guarantee they'd fit the Zenith radio, though. Sometimes parts that looked like they'd match up perfectly turned out not to fit at all.

But it worked. The new tubes slid into place like they belonged there.

Before screwing on the back panel of the Zenith, I checked everything one more time, then plugged it in. Then I stood there admiring the radio. Whenever I was pretty sure a radio was fixed, I liked to wait a minute before turning it on. It was like closing a really good book just before the final page to make it last.

Now to check. I turned on the radio for a few seconds, then switched it off and stepped back. No smoke, so I hadn't blown anything up. Nothing in the air but the smell of old radio. My favorite smell. It reminded me of attics and campfires and the antique books in Mr. Gunnar's store. I'd read that the smell was just radio parts and dust warmed up by electricity, but it was more than that. It was like the radio was remembering every home it had ever been in.

I reached over to turn it back on, then placed my hand on the speaker. Static hummed against my fingers. Almost there. The slightest turn of the knob, and the vibrations smoothed out. There was the music.

Usually I didn't think about what music sounded like. But right then, with my hand on the radio, I wondered if any note of the song vibrating the speaker sounded like Blue 55.

At my computer I searched for more about the whale. A website about whale migration came up, with maps showing where different species of whales swam throughout the year. A lot of whales were hanging around California or Alaska for the summer since that was where the food was. When it got colder they'd swim back to Hawaii or Mexico or some other warm place.

The most interesting part was how the scientists made those maps. A few whales had trackers on them, like the one that Andi from the sanctuary tried to put on Blue 55. But the scientists knew where most of the whales were because of underwater microphones in oceans all over the world. They listened to the songs and knew what kind of whale sang them. Then they'd add to the map, showing a humpback pod in Massachusetts or a minke whale in Norway. The whales' songs were like footprints they left in the ocean.

This worked even if the whales were far away. Sound traveled farther in water than in air, so a whale song could be heard from hundreds of miles away, maybe more.

Blue 55 had a map all his own. He traveled the same waters as some other whales, but at different times. Sometimes there were gaps in his route, when no microphone picked up his song. Either he wasn't singing then or other noise in the ocean drowned out his calls. A dotted blue line on the map showed the best guess of where he was.

Sometimes he took a completely different route, one that no other whale ever did. The lines on the other whales' maps were smooth, curving up or down coastlines. Blue 55 took a more jagged route. He'd start swimming one way, then for some reason change direction and go off to the side or back the way he'd just been.

I traced the blue line with my finger. *What are you looking for?*

Below each map was a recording of the whales' songs. When I clicked on a sound file, colored lines on a graph rose and fell, showing the volume and frequency of the songs that played.

I ran downstairs to bring up the website on Mom's computer, since it had speakers plugged into it. With the volume turned up, I rested my hand on a speaker and clicked on each sound file. The low calls of the normal whales vibrated more strongly against my hand than 55's did. It didn't feel like a huge difference, though. I wished I could understand the songs and figure out what they were saying, or at least why they couldn't talk to one another.

I couldn't imagine trying for so long to reach out to someone else when there was never a reply. Either he was still waiting for someone to answer back or hearing his own song was enough for him.

With my hand on the computer's speaker, I closed my eyes as the song fluttered against my fingers. This was different from anything I'd felt through a radio speaker before. Not like any other music, and not like talking, either.

A steady vibration tickled my palm as Blue 55 sang out a long call that seemed like it would never end. Then the speaker pulsed when he switched to short bursts of sound. While keeping one hand on the speaker, I placed the other over my heart to feel the matching rhythms of my heartbeat and the whale song.

On another website, I found a picture of Blue 55, taken by a photographer with an underwater camera. It looked like one of the images from the video Ms. Alamilla showed us. A profile of his face, with the black oval of his eye centered on the photo. It hadn't been so long ago that I first saw him in that video, but it felt like I'd always known him. I clicked print on the photo so I could tack it to my wall.

While the printer ran I swiveled the chair around to the window and watched Tristan and his friends playing basketball in the driveway. My eyes darted from one to the other, trying to grab any scrap of conversation as they dribbled and passed the ball and shot baskets. They all laughed and high-fived their friend Pablo over something he said. Tristan aimed for the hoop but then started laughing again, doubled over this time.

I turned back to the printer. The guys were probably laughing about something dumb anyway.

When I clicked on the sound file again, one hand felt the song playing through the speaker, and the other hand held a picture of who was singing.

12

Mr. Gunnar smiled and waved when I carried the Zenith into the shop. I set it on the counter and waited while he rang up a customer buying a creepy old doll.

"It really works?" he said after the customer left. Mr. Gunnar used to have such a bushy mustache that talking to him was like trying to lip-read a walrus. He kept it trimmed now so it didn't hang over his upper lip anymore.

I nodded and invited him to check it out. Sometimes the radios needed a little more adjusting after I thought I was finished. I knew when a radio was working, but couldn't always tell if the sound was clear enough. Some static was too faint for me to feel crackling against the speakers.

Mr. Gunnar's smile let me know I got it right. He shook his head and laughed, then he looked at me so

I could see his mouth. To make things clearer he threw in a few signs he'd learned from me.

"I admit, I wasn't sure you could fix this one." He tied a price tag to the cord, then handed me the radio. After putting it on a shelf, I wandered around the store to see if there was anything I needed. Mr. Gunnar gave me an employee discount, even though I wasn't an official employee.

That store was where I first got interested in electronics. Grandpa and I would pick up things like old lamps and toys and take them home to work on them together. Sometimes we'd take parts from different lamps and make a whole new one, like the bottle lamp I made for Grandma. Then I started not just fixing things, but making things. I built an alarm clock that shook my mattress in the morning, all with parts I picked up at Moe's. I made an alarm clock for Tristan, too. He could hear just fine, but he was such a deep sleeper, nothing could wake him. At first I gave him an alarm clock I'd connected to a truck horn. It did wake him up, but it also woke my parents, who said they nearly had heart attacks when it went off. I made him another one out of an old toy police car that drove around his room blaring its siren until he got up to turn it off.

One day when Grandma and Grandpa were shopping for furniture, I discovered the radios. I pushed buttons and turned knobs, trying to figure out how they worked. Mr. Gunnar took the time to explain what he could, pointing at radio parts and jotting down notes on some scrap paper. Even better, he gave me a broken old radio to take home to work on. After he handed it to me and saw how excited I was, he held up a hand like he had to warn me of something. *It'll be a challenge,* he wrote.

Well, that did it. I didn't know whether he meant that it'd be a challenge for *anyone* to repair that radio, or for me because I wouldn't hear when it started working. Either way, I was taking it home. Lately I'd been feeling like I could fix anything. I was ready for a challenge.

He added to the note, *The best way to learn how something works is to take it apart and put it back together.* I don't know what made him think I was smart enough to do that, but he did.

It took a lot of work, and I almost gave up a few times, but eventually, I did get that radio fixed. More importantly, it taught me how radios worked. I'd lost count of how many I'd repaired since then. I would've missed out on all that if I hadn't been there with my grandparents that day. Without that store and Mr. Gunnar, I wouldn't know I was good at anything.

After shelving the Zenith, I didn't find anything I needed, so I went back to the front counter empty-handed. As Mr. Gunnar wrote out the check for my repair payment, something in the display case caught my eye. I held up a hand to stop him, then tapped the glass over the item. He smiled and pulled a giant key ring from his pocket so he could unlock the case, then looked at me to see if he was removing the right thing. I held out my hand, and he placed the gold circle on my palm.

It looked like an old pocket watch. Etched into the cover was an ocean scene, with a whale leaping out of the water next to a sailing ship.

With a fingertip I traced the black outline of the whale. Mr. Gunnar reached over and unlatched the cover, revealing not a watch but a compass.

"Still works," he signed.

A compass. Even better than a watch. I closed the cover and ran my finger over the etching again, wondering about who it had belonged to. A ship captain, I guessed, because of the design. Before computers and GPS, people navigated with compasses and the stars in the sky.

Finding that whale compass felt like a good sign. Like maybe it'd bring me good luck in figuring out a way to talk to Blue 55. I held it up to let Mr. Gunnar know to subtract the price from what he owed me.

"Something different!" he said, then signed the check. "Ready to sell me that Philco?" he asked before I left. He didn't need to sign or write that down because he asked that every time. He was sort of teasing. Sure, he'd love to have the Philco back, but he also knew I'd never part with it.

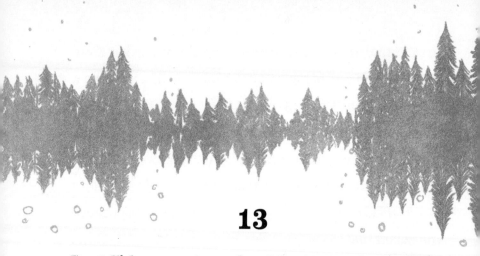

13

Wendell's house was just a short bike ride from Mr. Gunnar's shop. Before leaving home I'd stuffed my notes about frequencies and piano keys into the front pocket of my jeans.

Wendell's nine-year-old sister, Eleanor, was practicing tennis in the driveway as usual, a bundle of black braids flying behind her as she served a ball to the garage door and chased after it for the return. One got past her, and I grabbed it as it rolled toward the street.

"Looking good," I signed after tossing it back to her. Eleanor's goal was to be a better tennis player than Venus and Serena Williams put together. Not just because they'd be old by the time she could play them. She wanted to be good enough to beat them any time.

She set the ball and racket down to free up her hands. *"Thanks. Getting ready for a match this weekend."* Eleanor signed like a Deaf person even though she was hearing. Wendell was the only one in their family who'd ever been deaf, as far as anyone knew. Their parents started learning sign language right after Wendell was born, and they signed all the time at home. His mom was even a teacher of the deaf at Bridgewood Junior High, where Wendell would go next year.

"You'll do great. Wendell here?"

She pointed into the house while taking a gulp from her water bottle. Summer had hit Houston already, and Eleanor's brown face was shining with sweat. *"He's changing the stars,"* she signed after setting her bottle back down.

Through the glass panel on the front door, I saw the flicker of the strobe light when I pressed the doorbell, followed by the tall figure of Wendell's mom. We had a flashing doorbell at home too so I'd know when someone was at the door. I'd wired mine so that lamps in the living room and my bedroom blinked on and off when someone rang the doorbell.

Ms. Jackson answered the door and smiled. *"Great to see you,"* she signed. *"Wendell's upstairs."*

I thanked her and ran up to Wendell's room, where he stood on a wooden ladder, pulling sticky plastic stars from the ceiling. His T-shirt read "You Are Here," with an arrow pointing to a spot in the Milky Way.

I didn't have to ask what he was doing; he was always rearranging the stars to match the current night sky.

He gave me a one-handed *"What's up?"* with the hand that wasn't holding a star chart.

"Can I play the piano?" I asked.

"Probably not very well."

I put a hand on one hip and signed, *"I'm serious,"* even though I was trying not to laugh. *"I mean, I want to check something out on the piano."*

He climbed down from the ladder and led me into his family's library, which was also their piano room.

We sat on the bench together and he asked, *"So what's the thing you have to check out?"*

I handed him the slip of paper from my pocket.

"It's about this whale."

"What kind of whale?"

"Not a kind of whale, just one specific whale. I learned about him in science." I placed a hand on top of the piano, and Wendell did the same thing.

At the top of the page I'd written *regular whales 28 Hz, 1st piano key. 35 Hz, 5th key.* With one finger I struck the key on the far left. The low sound vibrated against my palm. I played it a few times so we could get to know the sound. Then I did the same thing with each key up to the fifth one, a black one that played thirty-five hertz. Blue and fin whales didn't sing much higher than that.

On the next line of the page I'd written *55 Hz, 13th piano key*.

I counted over starting from the first key, until I landed on number thirteen, a white key this time. I played the note a few times, and the vibration tickled my palm again, a bit lighter than the others.

"So this whale," I explained to Wendell. *"That's what he sounds like."* I hit the key again. *"But here's what he's supposed to sound like."* I struck the first key again. *"So he can't talk to other whales."*

Wendell placed both hands on top of the piano, as I alternated between the two notes. *"Not much of a difference,"* he signed.

"It's a big difference for whales."

He was right—it didn't feel like much of a difference. Less than a foot apart on the keyboard, but it separated Blue 55 from all other whales. I thought back to my visit with Grandma and how we sat right next to each other on the couch and couldn't think of what to say.

The befuddled face of Wendell's father peeked into the room. He looked like a taller version of Wendell, but with a bald brown head instead of a buzz cut.

Wendell raised his arms so his dad could see his signs over the top of the piano. *"It's our new act. We're going on the road as dueling pianists."*

"It'll be great." Mr. Jackson laughed and added, *"As long as your audience is deaf too."* Wendell rolled his eyes like he was annoyed, but then laughed too. His dad was used to signing all the time, and he could jump in on any conversation with us. Wendell told me before that he'd gladly trade for a dad who didn't say anything unless he had to, but I knew he didn't mean it.

"So he can't sing lower or something?" Wendell asked after his dad left.

"No. He's been swimming around by himself for a long time, so I think if he could talk to other whales, he would."

"Or he's a loner and doesn't want to." Wendell nudged my shoulder. I didn't ask him why.

"I don't know, maybe. I think he just can't."

"And other whales can't hear him?"

"If they can, they don't know what he's saying."

I played each note again, focusing on the difference, and wished I could lower the piano into the ocean and play that note for Blue 55. *"I want to find a way to talk to him."*

"To the whale?"

"Yes, the whale."

"How?"

"That's what I have to figure out."

"Then what?"

"I don't know that, either. Not yet."

We took turns playing the keys, while each of us rested a hand on the piano.

"Why do you want to talk to him?" Wendell asked.

I didn't know how to answer him, how to explain that this whale swam in an ocean surrounded by other whales he couldn't talk to, that there was no pod or single whale who understood him—not even his own parents—and that I wanted to create a song that would let him know he wasn't alone. I couldn't fully explain it to myself, either. I tried to come up with something to compare it to, like the pull of a tide, or something Wendell would understand better, like the gravity of a black hole drawing in everything around it.

"He keeps singing this song, and everything in the ocean swims by him, as if he's not there. He thinks no one understands him. I want to let him know he's wrong about that."

14

A pod of humpbacks swam past. He hadn't met them before; he was sure of that. He would remember. A whale remembers everything, even the things he tries very hard to forget.

Maybe he could join them. He approached from the side, swimming at the edge of the migrating family. For a time he would hang back, gliding silently alongside them. Later, if they didn't object, he would drift closer.

He had tried this before, each time hoping he would be allowed to stay, even if they couldn't understand his music. The pods who'd recently lost a member were the easiest to join. He knew them by their songs made of low, mournful tones, announcing their grief to the ocean. They swam with an empty space, carrying the shadow of a whale who used to be. Whether they craved a new whale to fill the emptiness or didn't have the strength to slap a tail to tell him to leave, he didn't know.

He created music the same way they did: forcing breath into spaces in his body, circulating the air until breath and space turned into song.

Still, the sound wasn't right. The tones didn't match the ones around him.

They had heard. He knew by the way they glanced back. With time, maybe they would understand just one sound, the smallest ripple of his song. And that would be enough.

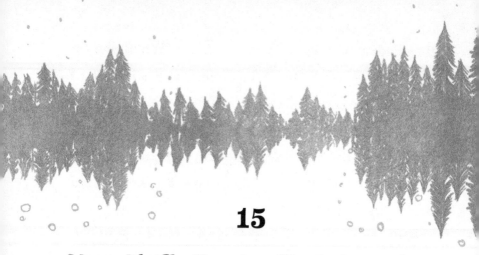

15

I dreamed that Blue 55 sang to me. When I woke up, my hand still rested on top of the Philco.

Maybe the radio station had been playing a song with notes that hit fifty-five hertz. I wanted to feel them again. But the vibrations from the radio had changed to the choppy rhythm of talking, and the whale song from my dream had slipped away.

After that I couldn't fall back to sleep. I kept thinking about Blue 55's song, and wanted to feel it again. A search on my phone took me to an article called "Making Music with Whales," which had pictures of weird sheet music. I'd had to sit through enough music classes in elementary school to know what it should look like. Instead of black dots or circles for each note, these pictures showed music scales with colored lines and shapes over them. At first glance it looked like someone had splattered paint, making a colorful chain of islands across the page. As I looked more carefully, the shapes became more defined. One shape looked like a wobbly heart, another like a bird.

Sheet music for whale songs. Maybe I'd found a way to understand the whales' music without hearing it.

The colored splotches and lines represented the parts of the songs. Plain black dots weren't enough to show what a whale song sounded like. They sang more complicated songs than humans could compose. The colorful splotches covered more of the music scale than human music, with different notes flowing together in each part of the song.

The humpback's songs were the most complex, with lots of colors and shapes dancing up and down the musical scale. The songs of most whales stayed near the same lines of the scale instead of zigzagging from very low to very high, and didn't have as many colors. It was like most whales were playing one instrument and the humpbacks played a whole symphony. Their sheet music showed a song with an orange-pink-purple-red-and-blue pattern over and over, but the whales stretched them out as they went on, before starting the song over again with short bursts of sound.

The article even had sheet music for Blue 55. Some

of the colors were the same as the other whales', but they were higher on the musical scale and in a different pattern. His song was in a blue-purple-and-red pattern, adding a part at the end of each section that looked like wavy lines on the sheet music. Sometimes those waves were blue; sometimes red or purple. But he'd always sing the wavy-line part of the song before starting the pattern over again.

Same shape, different colors. Like Grandpa's poems—the same handshapes but different signs. Blue 55's own rhyme.

The notes on the page swirled together with the plan I'd started thinking of before I went to Wendell's to play the piano.

I found a chart online that listed musical instruments and the frequencies they played. Not many instruments could get as low as fifty-five hertz. Even though it was a high sound for a whale, it was low for humans. The tuba could play it, and the bass trombone. And a harpsichord, whatever that was. I printed out the chart, along with the sheet music.

I tacked Blue 55's song next to his picture on the wall. The song wasn't like any other, and no other whale understood it. But it was his. Maybe it didn't look like much on paper, but there was another way it was like Grandpa's poems: the whale needed space above and below and all around him to sing his song.

When I was in third grade, I had to go to music class with my homeroom. We followed a rotation for PE, library, music, and art. I had to be dragged out of the library when it was time to leave. In art I could paint or draw what I couldn't say. PE was something to put up with. But in music I would daydream while the class learned about musical notes or whatever, or I'd have to sign the songs along with Mr. Charles. The day the teacher handed out recorders for us to play, I asked Mom to get me out of the class. Playing music was worthless. From then on I had extra library time when the rest of my class went to music.

Then there I was, at the end of my sixth-grade year, standing in front of a door that read MUSIC ROOM. That morning I'd stopped by to ask the music teacher, Mr. Russell, if I could talk to him about a project. He said he'd have some time after school.

Before opening the door, I reached up and touched the whale compass, which I'd been wearing as a necklace. The day I brought it home from Mr. Gunnar's,

I dug through my jewelry box for a gold chain. Everything was either too short or the wrong color, except the one around my neck holding the radio knob. I unhooked the chain and threaded it through the loop at the top of the compass. As I hooked the clasp around my neck, I wondered if that ship captain who owned it ever found his way home.

A message on Mr. Russell's whiteboard read *Back after bus duty.* While I waited I browsed the posters of instruments on the walls. I pulled my notes about musical instruments and frequencies from my pocket, then touched the holes on the picture of the bass saxophone on the "Brass" poster. Someone who knew which holes to cover or uncover while blowing into the instrument would be able to play a note that Blue 55 would hear.

Mr. Russell waved his hand near me to let me know that he was back, then said, "Hooooow caaaaan I heeeellllp yoooou?"

Normally his slow, exaggerated talking would annoy me, but my excitement about my plan pushed that aside. I handed Mr. Russell my notes, along with the sheet music for Blue 55's song. At the bottom of the page I'd written *I want to record a song for this whale.* He sat at his desk to look over everything, then flipped back to the beginning and read it again. I didn't notice until he glanced at my hand that my fingers were drumming his desk.

When he started to talk, I handed him a marker and pointed to the whiteboard.

Fascinating, he wrote. *I can put something together for you with some of the band and orchestra students. It won't sound so good to humans, but it could be a big hit for whales.* He laughed.

With a red marker I wrote, *Thanks. When can I come back to record it?*

A few students were coming into the music room with their instrument cases.

Tomorrow after school? he wrote. *It won't take long since it's only a couple of notes, just oddly played.*

Perfect. Once I got a sound file of the recording, I'd have the biggest part of what I needed. The plan to reach out to Blue 55 was coming together.

I smiled and wrote *Thank you!* on the board before leaving.

Mr. Russell hadn't asked what class my project was for, or even if it was for a class at all. That was okay. This was more important than any class.

Dear Andi,

Thanks for answering my questions so fast. Can you send me a recording of the sanctuary's animals, for a project I'm working on?

If you could send me a sound file of whatever you record, that would really help.

Thanks,

Iris Bailey

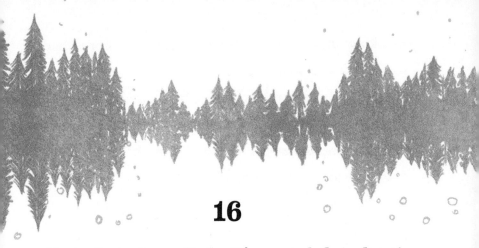

16

The students who would play 55's song took their places in the music room the next day. Many of the students sat off to the side to observe. Even the lowest notes of violins, clarinets, and trumpets were too high for Blue 55. I was surprised a tuba player wasn't participating. That was one of the few instruments I'd listed, since it could play notes even lower than 55's. But Mr. Russell said that the note I needed was hard to play, and he didn't have a student who could do it. So it took more skill than I'd thought, if you couldn't just play the note by holding your hands in the right place and blowing into the mouthpiece alone.

Before you leave I'll show you a way you can create that sound on a phone or tablet, he wrote on a sticky note.

Listed on the whiteboard were the instruments participating and the notes they'd play. I waited in a chair at the front of the room while the group did a couple of practice rounds. It looked like the students were checking something on their phones or some other small device after playing a note, sometimes shaking their heads and playing again. Mr. Russell played the piano and pointed to each student in turn, directing them to play the notes that matched fifty-five hertz. They played the ones just above or below that, too, since Blue 55 sometimes sang a little higher or lower. A few students watching the performance covered their ears. Hopefully it would sound better to 55.

Behind the rows of blue plastic chairs were the students with larger instruments. A boy with shaggy blond hair played the bass saxophone. I recognized Angelica Freeman because she lived a few houses down from me. She moved the fingers of one hand along the neck of an upright bass, the instrument I'd always thought of as an overgrown violin. Her other hand worked the bow back and forth across the strings.

After a few minutes Mr. Russell said something to the group, then stood up from the piano bench and wrote *Ready for the real thing* on the board. Mr. Russell turned on the microphones and stereo equipment. Later he'd email me the recording of the song.

If the room didn't have deep wall-to-wall carpet, I could have taken off my shoes to feel the vibrations of the music, like of the bass drum that sat on the floor.

I wondered what all those instruments sounded like together, then reminded myself it was like the song of 55 I'd felt on the computer speakers at home. I just wished I could feel it then.

Instead of sitting down again after pressing the record button, Mr. Russell pointed to me, then to the piano bench.

I pointed to my chest. *"Me?"*

He nodded, then wrote, *It's your song. Only fair you get to play it.* I smiled and sat at the bench. Playing Blue 55's song was even better than hearing it. Mr. Russell made a tapping motion near the correct key, but I already knew which note to play. I placed a finger on the thirteenth key, then looked up to wait for his cue.

When he waved his hands, I tapped the piano key over and over, while the other students played their notes. I played the twelfth and the fourteenth keys also, to add the sounds just above and below fifty-five hertz.

Mr. Russell raised a hand, then made a fist. After we paused the recording, everyone applauded, even the students who'd been covering their ears. Maybe they were just clapping because it was over, but I didn't mind. We had the song that would tell 55 someone was out there.

As the students took their seats for their regular

practice, Mr. Russell showed me an app on his tablet. He held the phone near the piano and pointed to the thirteenth key. When I tapped it, the phone's microphone picked up the sound. Wavy lines appeared on the screen, along with the name of the note: A1. Best of all, a readout of the frequency, fifty-five hertz, appeared next to the sound wave with each strike of the key. Mr. Russell pointed to the students to show me that they were using similar apps. That was how they knew if they hit the right note. Already I felt closer to Blue 55, from playing that sound like the one he sang.

Mr. Russell showed me how to adjust a wheel on the screen to select any musical instrument. That was what he meant when he said I could play the tuba note myself. He spun the wheel to "Tuba," then showed me which note to tap. Purple lines of a sound wave, and "55 Hz" appeared in the middle of the screen. I should've known there'd be an app that would allow me to play the song. Instead of working with the music students, I could have created the song myself. But it wasn't so bad, working with them. Now that they knew about Blue 55 too, it was like he had more people listening to him.

Before I left, I drew a smiling whale on the whiteboard saying "Thanks everyone!" Some of the kids smiled and waved to me as I left, and Angelica gave me a thumbs-up.

Okay, maybe playing music wasn't worthless.

While I waited at home for Mr. Russell to finish band practice and email me the file, I tried out the tuner app he'd showed me. I worked in the study so I could use the computer speakers. Usually Mom worked at home doing graphic design, but that day she was at a meeting with a company she did some work for.

Whenever I found a note that was around fifty-five hertz, I recorded the sound on the computer. I scrolled through the selection of instruments, some of which I'd never heard of, like the euphonium. By playing with the plus and minus buttons marked "Octave," I got a few more instruments to hit the right sound. I threw in a few notes from fifty to sixty hertz to give Blue 55 a little variety.

How long could practice go on? Just when I was thinking Mr. Russell had forgotten about me, the email came through.

I opened the attached file and hit play. The vibrations coming from the speaker reminded me of 55's song. Maybe it would remind 55 of his song too.

The other sound files I needed were in a new email
from Andi.

Dear Iris,

Great to hear from you again. I made underwater
recordings today with the hydrophones, and I've
attached the file here. Often it's noisier than what
I recorded for you, but we don't have any cruise
ships coming in today, so it's mostly natural sounds
here, such as humpback and blue whales, orcas,
seals, and the wind on the ocean surface.

Good luck with your project. I'm interested in
hearing more about it.

Andi

Yep, you'll be hearing about it, Andi.
The recording was only about five minutes long. I'd
have to do some editing so Blue 55 would have a longer song to listen to. After I dragged the clips from Mr.
Russell and Andi into a new file, I copied them over
and over so they'd replay for an hour.

Hopefully it would be enough. I placed my hand over
the speaker and closed my eyes while the song played.
I'd thought before that playing 55's real song wouldn't
do any good because he'd recognize it as his own, but I

wondered what would happen if it was mixed in with this new music. I added a clip of Blue 55's recording to the middle of the song I'd just arranged.

There ... Something familiar yet different; a bit of his own song woven in with the new one. It was impossible to make the song exactly like 55's, but I did my best to stretch out the notes or clip them so they'd match the pattern of his music. I'd read that whale songs were made up of units, like single moans, chirps, or cries put together to build phrases. A bunch of phrases made a theme. Like spoken words that make up sentences and then paragraphs. Or like signs that made up phrases, then conversations or poems or stories. Maybe 55 would know this story was for him.

After all that work, I had to sit there for a while to figure out my reply. This would be the most important message I'd ever written. It had to be just right.

Dear Andi,

Thanks so much for sending the recording of the sanctuary animals. It's just what I needed for my project.

I haven't stopped thinking about Blue 55 since I first learned about him from my science teacher, Sofia Alamilla.

My hands hovered over the keyboard. I wanted to tell her my plan without making it seem like I thought I was smarter than the sanctuary staff.

> Since it didn't work out last time you tried to put a tracker on him, I thought you might like this idea I came up with.

I told her how I'd worked with the musicians at school to record a song at Blue 55's frequency, and then mixed it with his own song and the sounds of the sanctuary animals.

> A sound file of the song is attached here. What you could do is play it while you're on the boat, and plug a set of waterproof speakers into whatever device you're using. Then you can drop the speakers into the water, and 55 will hear the song. You said he swims to other whales, right? And they're not even singing the same songs. I'm sure when he hears something that sounds like him, he'll follow, and he'll want to hang around for a while.

I thought about how whenever I was with another Deaf person, we'd take forever saying our goodbyes. It annoyed everyone else as they stood in the doorway waiting for us to finally say goodbye and mean it. We'd almost get there, then think of something else to tell each other. If you don't know when you'll get to talk to someone like you again, you don't want your time together to end.

Whenever he's near your sanctuary, this song can help him feel at home. Maybe other sanctuaries could play it too, like when he migrates to warmer areas. He won't feel so alone hearing something like himself out there.

I don't know how many times I reread that email to make sure it looked right. It had to be professional, but casual, too, as if we sort of knew each other and were working for the same thing. I kept editing the message, changing words here and there and then changing them back again. Finally I did it. I held my breath and clicked send.

Your song is on the way, Blue 55.

17

I wanted to see Wendell in person to update him about the whale song. After school the next day, I called on the videophone to ask if I could come over. He said if I hurried, I could ride with him and his mom to the junior high. Ms. Jackson had been absent from work that day because of some meetings, so she wanted to stop by her classroom to prepare for the next day.

On the long drive to Bridgewood Junior High, I told Wendell all about recording Blue 55 a song and sending it to the sanctuary.

"That's so cool! Did you hear back yet?"

"Not yet. It hasn't been that long, though." I tried not to worry about not getting a message from Andi yet. Even though it hadn't been a whole day, I kept checking my email for a reply. What if my idea really wasn't that great? Just because the song would be at 55's frequency, that didn't mean it would make sense to him.

An image popped into my head of Nina's waving hands asking a whale, *"Hey, how's the plankton?"* Creating something that annoyed Blue 55 would be worse than not making the song at all.

The junior high started later than we did, so students were still in class when we got to Bridgewood. On the way to Ms. Jackson's classroom, I stopped and backed up when some signing hands in a science classroom caught my eye. An interpreter signed to one group of students at a tall black table as the teacher talked to them. They weren't the only Deaf students in the room. At another table three students signed to one another as they worked. I wanted to jump in on the conversation about the electrical circuit they were building. Ms. Jackson went on to her class while Wendell waited for me in the hallway.

A woman approached the Deaf students and signed to them. It didn't seem like she was an interpreter. She just joined in on their discussion and asked what they'd do next.

"Who's that woman?" I asked Wendell.

"Ms. Martinez. The classes with a lot of Deaf students have a Deaf ed teacher in the room along with the regular teacher."

"She signs like a Deaf person."

"Probably because she's Deaf."

"They have Deaf teachers here?"

"Yeah, a few."

Wendell took my hand and pulled me away from the science class. Two students walked by us in the halls, signing with each other. They waved hi to Wendell as they passed.

I'd known that most Deaf kids went to Bridgewood, but I didn't expect to see so many. They'd be able to sign with one another all the time, like during class or PE games or in the hallways. At the lunch table.

Ms. Jackson was leaving her classroom with some books and a file folder when we got there.

"I'm going to the workroom to make copies for tomorrow's lessons. You two can wait here."

Everyone in the room knew Wendell since he'd been there with his mom before.

After he introduced me I wandered around and scanned the bookshelves while Wendell chatted with the other people in the room. A few kids sat at a half-circle table with another teacher who shared the room with Ms. Jackson. Other students worked at their own desks or computers. In one corner of the room, a TV topped with a videophone sat on a wheeled black cart.

I pulled a book from the shelf. It looked old, with just

a plain off-white cover, but it was the title that drew me in: *American Sign Language: A History*. I hadn't noticed Wendell standing next to me until he moved his hands.

"My mom uses that when she teaches Deaf history."

"Deaf history?"

"Yeah, it's interesting."

I'd never thought about Deaf people having a history or where our language came from. Wendell reached for the book and flipped to the beginning. I scanned the page he'd turned to, then read the caption beneath a picture of a white-haired man dressed in black, signing with a little girl.

"France?" I signed.

He nodded. *"Some French people came here and used their sign language to teach Deaf kids. There was just one school for a long time, so Deaf people from all over the country went there and shared their own signs with one another."*

"And that's the sign language we use now?"

"It took a while, and it changes all the time, but yeah, that became ASL."

A new language. From groups who couldn't understand one another at first. Why hadn't I known about that?

Maybe Blue 55 and I would understand each other, just a little. Just one sound.

Wendell was signing with the other students and the teacher, telling them about Blue 55. They looked over at me and signed things like *"Really?"* and *"That's great!"* The teacher asked, *"Will you let us know how it works out?"*

I told her I would.

The junior high wasn't even Wendell's school yet, but he interacted with the other kids as if he were already going there. Next year, as a student, he'd know even more people. It must have been like that for him all the time, being able to talk to people around him so easily.

I'd thought about asking Mom again if I could go to school at Bridgewood. She'd probably say no. I hadn't brought it up for a long time, because I didn't like the way her face changed when I did. Kind of like when we visited Grandma, and she held me a little longer and looked at me like I was going somewhere far away. Maybe I could try again to convince her that it would be better here, that this is where I belonged.

I set the ASL history book down so I could join the conversation with the other students, but I missed what Wendell had just signed. Then I missed what they answered back. Somehow they were all keeping up with whatever they were talking about. I tried to tell myself I was just a little lost because I'd been looking down at the book when they started their conversation. But if that were it, I'd be able to catch up right away. Instead, I felt like I was tumbling in the murky water of the Gulf after a wave knocked me over.

After watching their conversation for a minute, I picked up a little more. Wendell was signing faster than he usually did with me. That wasn't the only difference. A few of the signs he was using were new to me. No one else at the table looked confused.

They turned to me like they were waiting for me to answer a question.

I shrugged at Wendell. *"I didn't catch what you were talking about."*

One of the students waved me off and signed, *"Train gone, sorry."* I'd missed out, and it was too much trouble to catch me up.

Wendell laughed a little and signed, *"Oh, sorry. I forgot to sign like an old person for you."*

I flinched like he'd slapped me. The other students laughed with him. Wendell stopped when he saw my face, then gave the others a small head shake.

"Sorry," he signed.

"It's okay," I told him, even though it wasn't true. I put the ASL history book back on the shelf. Maybe I wouldn't fit in here after all.

Wendell tapped my shoulder. I'd been looking out the window of the van while Mrs. Jackson drove us back home. *"Are you mad? I'm really sorry. I don't really think about it. I just sign a different way with you than I do at Bridgewood. You do that too, right? Like you don't sign the same way with your dad as you do with your mom or grandma or me."*

Well, that didn't help, bringing up how I have to sign differently for Dad to understand. I shook my head to let Wendell know he didn't need to apologize. *"It's okay,"* I signed again. It wasn't really okay, but it also wasn't his fault. We didn't see each other every day, and I wasn't around other Deaf people our age like he was. Most of my conversations had been with my grandparents or with Mr. Charles. So I wasn't mad at Wendell for signing differently for me than he did with other kids. I was mad that he had to do it at all.

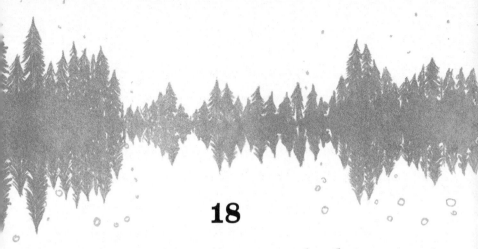

18

I was about to go downstairs for dinner when the message I'd been waiting for came in.

> Dear Iris,
>
> Sorry it took so long to get back to you. I was intrigued by your idea right away but wanted to run it by the rest of the team first. Great news—we will play your song for Blue 55 when we try again to tag him with the tracker!
>
> We'll also place a speaker in the deep waters of the sanctuary to see how he responds.

I couldn't believe it. That sanctuary staff all the way in Alaska had talked about me and the song I'd made. They liked my plan. I'd been afraid to hope they'd actually use it. Andi was a real scientist who cared about Blue 55, and she had listened to me.

This all depends on whether he's nearby, of course, and if we can find him. No one's heard him singing lately, so we're not sure where he is. Hopefully he'll start singing again if he's around.

Ask your parents for permission to give me your mailing address, and I'll be glad to send you a sanctuary T-shirt. We'll mention you on our Facebook page, and when it's time for the expedition to go out, click on the link to the live webcast so you can see your plan in action. And if you're ever around Appleton, Alaska (no one ever is, but just in case), stop by the sanctuary, and we'll give you a tour.

I'm so impressed by the work you've done. You're thinking like a scientist—you discovered a problem and worked out a way to solve it.

Thanks again for writing to us with your idea, Iris. We're looking forward to trying it out so we can learn more about Blue 55.

Andi

I was so excited that I jumped up and ran a circle around my room, stopping in front of the picture of Blue 55 on the wall. *I made a song for you. I hope you'll like it.* My hand brushed the picture of the whale's face, then dropped to my side. As happy as I was that

Blue 55 would hear the song, it didn't seem right to just watch online when it happened. While the sanctuary staff got to meet Blue 55, I'd be sitting at home in front of a computer screen. That wasn't enough. I should be there when he heard the song.

Dear Andi,

I'm so happy you're actually going to use the song! Even though Blue 55 has never heard it, it's a song he's looking for. I'm sure of it. Thanks so much for writing back and for inviting me to your sanctuary. I'll ask my parents if I can go soon so I can be there when Blue 55 is.

Can I join you on the expedition? I'll be glad to help out. That way you can focus on tracking him, and I'll take care of the speakers and the song. I've been working with radios for a long time, so I'm used to handling electronics stuff. It's almost the end of the school year, so nothing much is going on anymore because we're done learning things. And my parents won't mind me missing a few days of school for such an educational trip.

I didn't add that my school sure wouldn't mind if I missed a few days either.

I guess that's it for now. Let me know when you think Blue 55 will be there!

Iris

Maybe Andi was only being polite when she told me to stop by if I was ever in the area, but I was going. I would meet that whale.

As soon as we sat down to dinner, I told my family about Blue 55, how it all started with the video in Sofia Alamilla's class, and about Andi and her team that tried to tag him.

Mom interpreted some of what I said for Dad since he didn't understand everything. I tried to slow down for him, but I couldn't stop my hands from flying. Then I told them about all the work I did studying Blue 55's song and how I'd figured out how to make a new song for him with the music from school and the tuner app.

"*And...*" I signed that part slowly, and looked around the table to make sure I had their attention. "*Blue 55 should be near the sanctuary again soon. The staff will try to tag him again, and they'll play my song underwater so he'll hang around longer.*"

"*Really?*" Tristan signed. "*That's impressive!*"

"That's great you were able to help them," said Mom. "You must have worked really hard on that."

Dad still looked a little lost, but signed, "Yes, great!"

They did seem impressed, but I wasn't sure they really understood what a big deal this was. Maybe I hadn't gotten across how long he'd been swimming alone and that nothing else sang like he did.

They'd get it when I told them the best part. "And guess what? Andi—she's the woman who will tag him—thought my idea was so good, she invited me to visit the sanctuary!" I left out the part about her saying I should stop by for a tour if my family ever happened to be in Appleton, Alaska. That was good enough of an invitation for me. We had to go.

Mom and Dad gave each other a look like they were trying to figure out what to say. Sometimes they tried to talk without moving their mouths when I was nearby, so I couldn't read their lips. Now it looked like they were communicating silently, though.

"That was nice of her," signed Mom. "Maybe someday we'll take a trip to Alaska, and you can see the sanctuary."

"Someday" meant never. "But we have to go soon," I explained, "when the whale will be there."

"Don't worry," Dad signed. "He has other whales around him all the time, right?"

They'd totally missed the point. If they understood what a big deal this was, they'd take it seriously. This whale was finally going to hear a song like his own, and I'm the one who made it. I was ready to answer any questions they had about Blue 55 or the sanctuary or the song. They didn't ask about any of it. Dad probably hadn't even *caught* most of it. I should have explained it better. This was the most important thing I'd ever do, and it was turning out all wrong.

After a deep breath I forced myself to slow down when I answered Dad. This would work out if I could be less excited, more patient. *"But they can't understand him. That's the problem. Even when other whales are nearby they don't know what he's saying."* My hands showed Dad the swimming whale, all alone in the ocean. Singing, while nothing answered back. Then one day there was a song. A song like his. I turned to the side and held a hand up to my ear like I was hearing the song myself.

When I finished, Dad looked up like he was thinking about my explanation, then said, "Sounds like that whale needs speech therapy." He laughed at his own joke, then said something else with his face downward.

I waved to get his attention, then signed, *"What?"*

He took a spoonful of his chili and signed, *"Nothing."* That was one sign he knew well.

"It isn't nothing. You mean I'm not important enough to include."

He looked at Mom for an interpretation, but I signed to her, *"Don't interpret anymore."* Dad's chest heaved with a sigh, so he must have understood that part.

"What if you couldn't talk to anyone around you? What if you tried, but no one understood?"

Dad glanced at Mom again, but she just reached for her glass. The water in the glass shook when I slapped the table. Dad signed, *"I can't understand you. You need to slow down."*

I signed faster. *"It doesn't matter what I do. You don't understand anyway! What if your whole life was like this? What if you were that whale, in an ocean with no one to talk to?"*

He shook his head and went back to his dinner.

Mom signed to me, *"Sweetie, I'm sorry you're upset, but we can't just drop everything and go to Alaska. We'll watch the expedition online. You can invite Wendell over, and everyone will see how you helped the whale."* She added, *"I'll make popcorn,"* like that would make everything better.

"No, this isn't fair! I'm the one who made the song. It was my idea to play it for him. I'll help pay for the trip." I had no idea what a trip to Alaska would cost, but I had some money in the bank from my repair work.

No one said anything for a while, and then Tristan touched my arm. "Hey. It is great, what you're doing for that whale. The important thing is that he'll get to hear your song, right?"

"Yes, but I should be there when he hears it. I need to see him...."

"He isn't one of your radios."

"What?"

"The whale," Tristan signed. "I know you don't like to leave anything broken. Make sure that's not the reason you want to do this. You can't go in there and fix him like he's a radio."

"I know that!" I signed it like I was smacking the air. What was he even talking about? "But I have to go there! I want him to know that someone hears him."

I went on like that, not stopping to wipe the tears from my face, signing so fast that Tristan couldn't keep up with me. Maybe even Mom couldn't, but I didn't slow down. I didn't care anymore. I was like Blue 55, shouting into the void of the ocean, at a frequency too high for anyone to reach.

19

The new pod was leaving him.

The youngest of the group stayed back, swimming around him in a circle, then floating nearby as the others called him. The calf was too young to have found his own song yet. He called to the large whale who swam alone, trying out clicks and chirps and fragments of a howl. With time they might understand each other.

That worried the pod. They didn't want the strange sounds piercing the waters around them, didn't want their calf singing the song they didn't understand. It was dangerous. How would he alert them when he needed help?

The humpback family called out, determined to

leave yet unwilling to move on without the calf. With a final chirp, the young whale turned to join them.

For a moment the larger whale followed, knowing he wouldn't be allowed but not ready to let go. It had been so long since he'd sung with a calf. There had been others in his own family, back when he himself was a calf too.

The pod swam ahead, tails thrashing if he got too close.

If he had remained quiet, would they have let him stay? For a time he did hold on to his song, then revealed it little by little as his trust grew. The more he sang, the farther they drifted from him, and the tighter they encircled the calf.

A storm brewed in the ocean, but he wouldn't flee the area like the others. It was in storms that he sang loudest. He was like all the others then, unable to hear his song over the wind and the crashing waves.

He swam into the rough waters, bellowing his unheard songs into the void of the ocean. Maybe the churning and the pounding and the rolling water that carried his sounds away would rearrange them into a new composition another would hear.

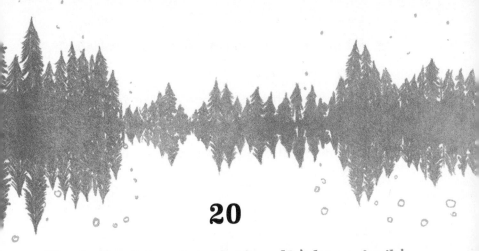

20

After I calmed down I decided I wouldn't let my family's response bother me. They just didn't get it yet. I'd firm up a plan with Andi, then try again with Mom and Dad. When they saw the proof that a real scientist was impressed by my idea and wanted me to come help out at the sanctuary, there's no way they'd say no. They'd see how important it was.

When an email from Andi came in later that night, I almost started packing a bag for Alaska. Then I read the message:

Dear Iris,

I'm so sorry if I gave you the idea that you should hop on a plane and fly here right now. That would be really hard for your family to do. It's a long way to go on short notice. (Plus, you might get here, and then there's nothing to see anyway, if Blue

55 doesn't show up. Sometimes science is kind of boring like that—you do a lot of planning and work, and then nature doesn't cooperate like you wish it would.) If your parents bring you sometime, that's great, but they'll want to take some time to plan the trip.

But please know that the view you'll have on a computer at home will be the same one the other members of the team will have, or even better! Tagging a whale is important work, but it is dangerous. We have to get really close to the whale to put the tracker on him. A slap from his tail could knock us out of the boat. Only one other person from the team will be out there with me, and that's the guy steering the boat. Everyone else who's been working on the expedition will be inside the sanctuary, watching on a video screen. Or they'll watch from outside on the dock, but they won't see much from there. You'll be able to see everything our cameras pick up from underwater and on the boat. Afterward I'll be happy to send you the information we get from 55's tracker. That way you'll know where he is and when he's singing, too.

Again, thank you so much for all the work you

did on this and for sending us the song. I'd love to talk to you more about it, and I hope we'll keep in touch. I know you're going to do great things, and I'll be interested in seeing what other work you do for animals in the future.

Andi

I yanked 55's sheet music off my wall so hard that the corners ripped and pushpins flew out of their holes. Before tearing the page to pieces, I stopped myself. It wasn't his fault. This was Blue 55's song. Whatever he was saying, whatever this language was, it was his.

Still, I wouldn't be able to look at it anymore. I folded it up, along with his picture, and buried it in the bottom drawer of my desk.

Wendell didn't have his own phone yet, so we had to chat online instead of texting. The chat window on the computer showed a red dot next to his name. I'd send a message anyway for him to read whenever he got online.

I heard back from the sanctuary. After that I didn't know what else to say. The dot next to his name stayed red as I sat there slumped in my chair. Finally I gave up and flopped into bed.

Mom came upstairs later to tell me that Wendell was on the videophone. I shook my head to let her know I'd talk to him another time. Lifting my arms to have a conversation would take too much effort.

A string of messages from Wendell was waiting for me when I got online the next morning.

What did they say?

Did they like your song? Are they going to play it?

Well??????

Are you alive????

In the chat window I typed, *Hey. Sorry, I didn't want to talk yesterday. But yeah, I heard back. They love my idea.*

I waited while he typed a response. *That's great! So then what was wrong yesterday?*

They invited me to visit sometime, and I want to be there to meet the whale. My parents say it's too far away. I'll get a T-shirt from the sanctuary. Oh, and a shout-out from the boat. While they're meeting the whale. Using the song that I gave them.

Wendell didn't type anything for a while, then wrote, *I'm sorry, Iris. That's not fair. It's your idea, right? So you should get to go.*

I'd gone to bed feeling like I'd never be happy again,

but I smiled a little then. Even though Wendell couldn't do anything to change what happened, it helped to have someone understand how unfair it was.

Thanks, Wendell. I'll be okay, I guess. But I'll be really mad about it for a while. They'll show the expedition online, but I don't think I'll watch.

Yeah, I wouldn't either. Well, come over again whenever you want. Jupiter and its moons will be visible soon.

Thanks, see you later.

Dad came in and sat on the edge of the bed while I was wrapping up my conversation with Wendell. He was holding a set of computer speakers.

When I swiveled my chair around, Dad pointed at the computer. I waved him over and stood next to the chair so he could sit.

He plugged in the speakers, then brought up a You-Tube video of an old record player. Not as old as the one in my Admiral set, but still pretty old. Instead of a round record like ones I'd seen, this had a square record spinning on the turntable. In the middle of the record was a line drawing of a humpback whale.

I placed a hand on the speaker as the record played. The vibrations reminded me of some of the whale songs I'd found online.

Dad opened up the notepad on the computer. His

typing was a lot faster and made more sense than his signing.

My parents got this in a magazine when I was a kid. He clicked back to the video and pointed to the title, "Songs of the Humpback Whale, *National Geographic, 1979."* Then he pointed to himself and pretended he was putting on headphones. *"Every day,"* he signed.

We sat there for a while, him listening to the whale songs and me feeling the song through the speaker, both of us watching the spinning record in the video. Dad raised and lowered his hand to show me how the song flowed from low to high and back again, in waves. I remembered from the sheet music I'd looked at that the humpbacks were the symphony players. The description of the video said their sounds ranged from very low to very high. So didn't they sometimes hit fifty-five hertz? As they sang from twenty to one hundred to thousands of hertz, small parts of their songs had to sound like Blue 55's. I wondered if he ever recognized any of their sounds when he was close enough to hear them. A few notes of a song, at least.

Before this, no one knew they had such complex songs, Dad typed. *There used to be a lot more whale hunting. After hearing them, people protested against hunting whales. There was more to them than anyone knew.*

So their songs saved them. That was how powerful they were.

I wanted to find them too, he added.

"The whales?" I signed.

He nodded. *"That's how you sign it, like a letter Y?"*

"Yeah, see how it looks like the shape of a whale's tail?"

He held out his right hand, with just the thumb and pinkie sticking out. I showed him how to move the hand up and down in waves, to look like the tail of a swimming whale, while making a horizon with the other arm.

Maybe this was Dad's way of apologizing to me for what happened at dinner. I was still mad I wasn't going to get to go to Alaska to meet the whale, but this was something we'd be able to talk about. We'd never had that before—something we were both interested in. I hadn't thought that reaching out to Blue 55 would help me reach out to Dad, too. But that was before I knew he was interested in whale songs. He must have understood how important they were to me now, since he came up to my room to tell me how he used to listen to them.

I was about to ask him more about the songs on the record when he typed, *I wish you could hear them.*

I wanted to tell Dad that I could hear the whales,

just not in the same way he did. I didn't know how to explain that so he'd understand.

Every day I tried to forget about Blue 55. No more reading about whales or the sanctuary expedition. For a while I wore the wooden Zenith knob alone on my necklace, but I put the compass back on since I missed the weight of it resting on my chest. I still liked to think about the people who might have used it a long time ago to find their way.

Mr. Gunnar gave me his most hopeless case, an ancient radio that should have been left for dead ages ago. But I'd figure it out. With radios it was clear how the parts communicated. And whenever I fixed it, I'd know. That was how electronics were—either the thing worked or it didn't. There wasn't any guessing about that.

It took scientists a long time to figure out how whales make their sounds. They don't open their mouths and sing like people do. The singing happens inside the spaces in their bodies, by pushing air into their throats and sinuses.

When I reached into the radio, the old wire insulation crumbled into dust in my hands. Even if I got everything working, a bare metal wire could burn up all the work I'd done. I dug through the bundle of wires on my workbench, looking for replacements.

Was Blue 55 singing right then? Did anyone hear him?

I set the radio aside and went to my desk. My end-of-the-year research paper for Ms. Conn was due soon, and I hadn't started yet. I'd chosen radio communication as my topic, then asked her if I could change it to whales. Not that I didn't care about radios, but I could put all my whale research to use for my report.

If I asked to change my topic again, Ms. Conn's face would turn inside out with sour pickleness. But I couldn't write about whales anymore. When I turned it in, I'd tell her I'd changed my mind.

I brought up my favorite sites about radio history to take some notes. *FM radio signals can be detected thirty to forty miles away.*

That wasn't so impressive, now that I knew how far a whale song could travel. It could drift even farther than hundreds of miles. A song could reach up from the waves and halfway across the country, beating in time with someone's heart and pulling her to the ocean.

The sanctuary people finding him wouldn't be the same. Someone who heard him, who understood him, needed to be there.

I shook my head to clear away the thought. Then I shook out my hands too, trying to release the grip that Blue 55 had on me. There wasn't any point in thinking about him anymore. It would have to be enough that I'd helped him. I'd stick to what I was good at—fixing things—and forget all about that whale.

The website I brought up had examples of emergency communication using radios and telegraphs. I'd add one of the stories to my report.

One farmer connected his farm radio into his tractor battery when the radio's battery died. He heard the news about a coming storm just in time to get his family safely into the root cellar.

Then there was a shopkeeper who sent his daughter out of town to keep her away from the newspaper reporter she loved. After the reporter's "Matilda, please marry me" telegram reached her, they each took a minister to a telegraph station and were married by Morse code before Matilda returned home.

A soldier in a prisoner-of-war camp made a radio with a scrap of wood, a razor blade, a pencil, a safety pin, and a piece of wire from the fence surrounding the camp. At night he listened to reports about the war and passed the news along to his fellow prisoners.

I pulled 55's picture and sheet music from my desk

drawer where I'd hidden them, then tacked them back into place on the wall.

People who were desperate to communicate always found a way.

I'd find a way.

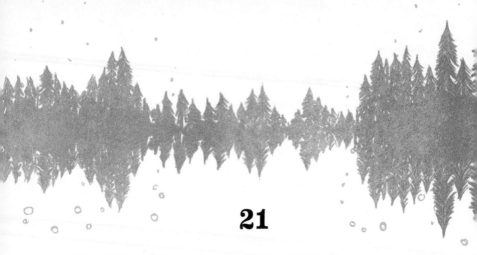

21

What if I could get there somehow? If I showed up at the sanctuary when it was time for the expedition, they'd see I was serious, that I wasn't just some kid doing a project. Even if I couldn't get on the boat, I'd be at the sanctuary when they tagged Blue 55. I'd see him swimming in the bay while the song played.

A twelve-year-old could fly alone. If I left in the morning on a school day, my family wouldn't notice I was missing until after I'd landed. But the closest airport was almost a three-hour drive from the sanctuary.

I studied the map on the computer screen. An airline ticket would let me cover almost all the distance between 55 and me. The hard part was the last 150 miles. If only I could grab on to 55's song and let it carry me to him. I was afraid one day soon I wouldn't feel his music anymore.

I didn't know how it would all work out yet, but I had

to try to get to him. I'd go as far as I could and then take a shuttle or a bus to get as close to the sanctuary as possible. Maybe I'd get caught by then. It wouldn't be hard for my parents to figure out where I was headed. But I couldn't give up on Blue 55.

Buying a plane ticket was a whole different issue. My radio repair money wouldn't take me very far. Even if I had enough, I'd have to buy the ticket with a credit card. I leaned back in my chair and glanced up at my shelves of radios, then sat on the floor next to my bed. An idea was creeping into my head that I didn't like but couldn't push away. I brought up 55's song on my phone, feeling the vibrations on my hand as it played. Hadn't I made him a promise?

With the edge of my shirt I polished my fingerprints off the side of the Philco.

My email to Mr. Gunnar was short, but it felt like it took me an hour to click send.

I'd always said I'd never sell my radios, except in case of an emergency.

I posted a few of the radios on eBay, as two-day auctions so the money would get into my account faster.

The next day after school, I hurried home to pick up the Philco. I wrapped it in an old bedsheet so it wouldn't get scratched. And maybe so I wouldn't have to look at it.

Tristan said he'd take me to the antiques shop. When he saw me in my room next to the sheet-wrapped radio he asked, *"Isn't that—"*

"Yeah," I signed before he could finish. *"Mr. Gunnar really wants to buy it. I don't mind letting it go."* I looked away so he wouldn't see how much the lie hurt. But at the same time, it was true. Letting go of the radios would let me reach for something I loved even more.

"Can you carry it for me? I'll wait in the truck." I slipped past him and ran downstairs.

Mr. Gunnar looked so happy when we walked through the door, he must have been worried I wouldn't show up. I couldn't really believe it myself.

When I was older I'd look for a Philco to buy again. Maybe from a kid like me who had a really good reason to sell it. An emergency.

I peeled away the sheet and held the sides of the cabinet one last time. Probably for a little too long, because Mr. Gunnar looked at me and raised his eyebrows like he was asking a question. I let go.

He knelt down and checked out the radio on all sides. His face showed me he was impressed. He plugged it in and turned it on, then smiled as he listened to the music.

Mr. Gunnar's open hand circled his face, then closed. *"Beautiful."* He thanked me and reached for his checkbook.

"Thank you," I signed to him before I left. I hurried out of the store ahead of Tristan, trying to outrun the thought that I could still change my mind.

"Wow, you really did it," Tristan signed when he got back into the truck.

"Can you take me to the bank?"

We pulled into one of the drive-through lanes, and Tristan put a deposit slip and the check into a plastic tube for me.

I ran my finger around the face of the compass and looked out the window, pretending not to notice Tristan staring at me. Then he tapped my arm, which I couldn't ignore.

"Sure you're okay?" he asked.

"Of course." I gave what I hoped was a convincing smile, and I sat back in my seat like I did this every day.

No big deal.

22

Later that week I stopped at the bank across the street from school. I'd gone with my mom or dad enough times to know what to do. My parents always showed a driver's license, which of course I didn't have, so I brought a copy of my birth certificate from Mom's desk. I'd get my money from my account, then go get some of those prepaid credit cards I'd seen on the racks at Walgreen's. I'd never paid much attention to them before, so I didn't know what amounts they went up to. I'd buy however many I needed until they added up to enough money for a plane ticket.

Instead of my usual outfit of jeans and whatever clean T-shirt I grabbed, I wore my black pants and a white shirt with buttons. I strode into the bank like it was totally normal for me to go in alone.

At the side counter I picked up a withdrawal slip and filled it out like I always did when I was with my parents. Except I was writing down a much bigger number than I ever had.

While I waited my turn in line, I told myself to quit fidgeting. I'd look nervous if I played with the corner of the withdrawal slip or fiddled with my necklace. Forcing myself to stand still with my hands at my sides made me look like a mannequin. I took a deep breath and imagined the vibration of Blue 55's song playing against my hands.

Finally the customer ahead of me finished whatever he was doing. I stepped up to the counter and handed the teller my withdrawal slip. I tried to look taller as she looked from the paper to me. She said something to me, and I guessed it was about an ID, so I unfolded my birth certificate and slid it over to her. She said something else I didn't catch, so I picked up the chained-up pen on the counter and motioned for her to write down what she wanted.

On the back of a blank deposit slip she wrote, *Are your parents here? One of them has to sign to withdraw money from this kind of account.*

I forced myself not to cry after I read the note. This was money I'd earned, from repair work and selling my radios. I should be able to take it out myself. I smiled like this wasn't a problem at all and wrote, *They're really busy with work and couldn't come. I'll have them sign it and come back later.*

After reading that the teller shook her head and added, *No, I mean they have to be here to show an ID and sign their name.*

I shoved the withdrawal slip and birth certificate into my backpack, then wrote on the note, *Oh right, I forgot. We'll come back later. Thanks!*

On my way out I smiled and waved at her, then signed something that would get me in Serious Trouble if anyone nearby knew sign language.

Now what? The whole point of parting with my radios was to have money to find Blue 55, and I couldn't touch it. Even if I asked my parents to withdraw some money for a radio or some parts, they would never believe I needed that much. When they'd noticed my missing radios, I told them I wanted to save up to buy more that needed fixing, since I liked repairing them. It was a little true, since I did plan to buy more radios when I had enough money. But right then, the whale was more important.

I got on my bike outside the bank but didn't turn toward home. I needed to talk to someone who understood me.

Grandma took her time answering the door, then gave me a hug and sat in her rocking chair by the window.

For a while I sat there looking out the window with her, staring at whatever she was always staring at. Nothing but trees and a parking lot, as far as I could tell.

Even though Grandma wasn't looking at me, I picked up my hands and poured out everything I'd been holding on to, all that I'd tried to do and failed at. I told her about Blue 55, the song I'd created, the trip I'd planned, the radios I'd sold, and the money in the bank I couldn't touch. Maybe it was so easy to let all that out because Grandma wasn't watching anyway, or because she'd understand how I felt. Maybe it was some of both.

But she should know that I needed her to see me, that there was a reason I went there to tell her all this. If she just looked my way, she'd see the pain on my face. I didn't expect her to fix it. She could just tell me she was sorry it happened. I'd feel better just knowing someone understood that disappointment and let me know that I'd be okay. Instead it was like I wasn't even there.

"And you know what else isn't fair?" I added, when she kept staring out the window. *"You're not the only one*

who misses Grandpa. But we can't all sit around being sad about him. Mom and Dad have to work, and Tristan and I have to go to school."

My hands finally dropped to my lap. I didn't know how to express the ache of getting so close to the whale and then missing him, as if he dove below the surface just as my fingers brushed the skin of his back. Maybe Grandma knew a sign for that kind of pain, but I didn't. It wasn't like the sign for *"hurt"* I use for a scraped knee or a headache, and it wasn't the twist at the heart that shows grief. Losing someone I'd never met wasn't the same as losing Grandpa. The closest thing would be the touch to the heart, like something piercing it. But that could also mean something that's touching or moving in a good way, because it's so beautiful.

Grandma turned to me and signed, *"What part of Alaska?"*

It took me a moment to realize she'd asked me a question. I didn't think she'd been paying attention at all.

"Oh, it's—" I held up a hand to represent the state of Alaska, then pointed at a spot along the southern coast—*"a little town called Appleton."* Not that it mattered anymore. Hopefully she saw enough to understand that I wasn't going. An ache crept into my stomach at the thought of explaining it again.

The night before, Mom came to my room to talk to me again about Blue 55. We'd avoided the subject since the dinner conversation that went so horribly wrong, and she was hoping to help me feel better. It didn't work.

Plus, she corrected me when I signed that I missed the whale, which annoyed me even more. I'd signed it with a touch to the chin; the *"miss"* sign for when someone you care about is gone. It didn't feel like the wrong sign. Even though I'd never met Blue 55, I did miss him. Mom showed me that the sign for *"miss"* I'd meant was the one with an open hand closing into a fist in front of the face, kind of like you're trying to catch a fly. The sign for something you tried to catch and couldn't, like when Blue 55 slipped away from Andi before she could tag him.

Yes, I was going to miss out on seeing Blue 55, but that wasn't what I meant. The *"miss"* sign I'd used was also like the sign for "disappointed," and I'd never understood why. Now it made sense. The meanings weren't so far apart. Someone you want to be with is far away, or something you wish for isn't going to come true.

"I know where that is," Grandma signed, pulling me back to our conversation.

"What, Appleton? How?"

"Some cruise ships stop there. I remember from when Grandpa and I were planning one."

Grandma and Grandpa went on cruises sometimes, but I didn't remember one to Alaska. "When did you go?"

"We were thinking about it for our anniversary next year."

I hadn't known they were planning an anniversary cruise. They almost made it fifty years.

"Grandpa always wanted to touch a glacier." Grandma didn't turn back to the window, but kept looking right at me. She hadn't done that for a long time.

I didn't know what to say to her about that cruise. I'd bring it up to Mom. Not because it would change her mind about going to Alaska soon—she'd made it clear that was ridiculous. But I'd try to convince her that we had to go someday. Not "someday" as in some imaginary time that would never come, but for real. I'd get to tour the sanctuary. Blue 55 wouldn't be there, but I'd see the place where he'd heard my song. And we'd find a glacier to touch, for Grandpa.

"Let's go," Grandma signed.

At first I thought she was thinking the same thing I was, that we could talk to my parents about planning a family trip. But Grandma didn't add *"someday."* Her chair wasn't rocking anymore. She leaned toward me, hands on the armrests of the chair.

"You mean ..." I couldn't finish the sentence, too afraid to hope for what she was suggesting. Even if I understood her correctly, I didn't see how it would work. Mom had already said we weren't going. It looked like Grandma had a different idea swirling in her head, though.

"So, what do you think?" she asked.

I shook my head and laughed, still not believing it. Like Andi said, Alaska is really far away, and people need time to plan a trip like that. But Grandma was one of those people who jumped into things like she did that day on the beach with the sei whale.

She didn't look away, and she didn't look like she was kidding.

Maybe I wouldn't have to miss out on meeting Blue 55. It would be for just a short time, a glimpse of him after such a long trip, but I'd have that to hold on to. And then I wouldn't miss him so much.

I squeezed Grandma's hand, then answered, *"I think it's time to get to sea."*

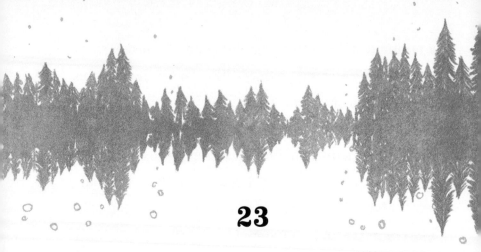

23

Grandma said not to worry about my money in the bank. *"Save it for something else. This is my treat."*

Instead of flying into the closest airport and trying to drive three hours, possibly through snow and ice, Grandma's plan was to get on a cruise ship that would take us right to Appleton.

We found just one ship with an available cabin and an Appleton stop, and we'd have to leave earlier than planned.

"How will we do it?" I asked. *"Like when it's time to leave, what will I tell Mom?"*

Grandma sat back to think, then picked up the activities calendar from her coffee table. *"We can't tell her what we're doing, exactly."*

"Right, there's no way she'd let us go. Not while I still have school, anyway."

"Or ever." Grandma pointed to her calendar, on the

date we needed to leave. *"Look, there's a day trip to Surf-side Beach. I'll tell your mom I'd like you to join me. It'd be good for us."*

"Think she'll say yes?" I couldn't believe we were actually planning this. It didn't seem real yet. More like a game. A really fun game.

Grandma shrugged. *"I'll talk her into it. We'll be with a group of people, and she knows how much I love the ocean. We'll be telling the truth about going to the beach anyway. We won't mention yet that we're going to one a little farther away."*

"A little?"

She looked back at the computer screen and clicked "Book my cruise." *"Just four thousand miles. No big deal."*

I smiled as I signed, *"Serious Trouble. We are both going to be in Serious Trouble."*

"Worth it," Grandma signed.

I couldn't leave without saying goodbye to Wendell. When I messaged to ask if he could come over, he wrote back, *Not unless you have a better telescope than I do. Come check out Jupiter.*

Mr. Jackson let me in at the front door and pointed upstairs. *"Great view up there."*

From the upstairs game room, I stepped out onto

the balcony and sat down next to Wendell. He didn't take his eye from the telescope until I touched his shoulder.

I reached down and clicked on Wendell's flashlight. He'd painted the lens red so the light wouldn't wash out the night sky and make the stars harder to see.

After the visit to the junior high, I'd wondered every day what Wendell was doing at his own school. Maybe he was learning the same things I was, but from a Deaf teacher, or he was signing with a bunch of friends at lunch, or joking with another student he passed in the hallway. If I were with them every day, I could be part of that. Even if we did sign a little differently, I'd sign more like the other kids after hanging around them more.

I shook the wish out of my head and tried to refocus. Changing schools would be impossible now. Mom wouldn't let me out of her sight again after she found out I took off to Alaska with Grandma.

I still couldn't believe Mom had said yes to the trip. I'd watched from upstairs when Grandma came over to talk to Mom about it. She kept a straight face the whole time and didn't give anything away. She really was a good actor. Before she left she got Mom to sign a permission slip. I held my breath as I backed into my room so Mom wouldn't hear me exhale. It felt like a loud sigh of relief I was holding in.

I looked up at the sky and asked Wendell, *"Which one is Jupiter?"*

"See that one that looks like a really bright star?"

"Yeah."

"But see how it doesn't twinkle like the stars?"

I hadn't noticed it before. What looked like a bright star was a solid light, not flickering like the others.

"If you see one like that," he continued, *"it's a planet. They're a lot closer than stars. It's all the atmosphere the stars' light has to travel through that makes them look twinkly."*

I looked through the telescope at the planet.

"That's awesome."

He pointed out the moons surrounding Jupiter. *"There's Io, Europa, Ganymede, and Callisto. It has a bunch more, but those are the ones we can see."*

While he took another turn looking through the telescope, I sat back and thought about what to tell him. I touched his shoulder again so he'd look at me.

"I have some news. About that whale, Blue 55. I'm going to go meet him after all. I'll try to anyway."

"Wow, really? That's great! Your parents changed their minds about going?"

"Well, no. They don't know about this."

"You're going by yourself?"

"With Grandma. She figured out a way we could get there. If Blue 55 shows up at the sanctuary, I'll be there to see him."

Wendell looked away and shook his head like he couldn't believe what I was telling him. I hardly believed it myself. It didn't seem real yet.

"And then what?" he asked.

"What do you mean?"

"I mean, after you find the whale. What will you do then?"

"I'm not sure. But I think the song will let him know he's not alone, and I want to be there for that."

Wendell didn't say anything for a while; he just stared at the sky. Maybe I'd made a huge mistake, and he was going to tell his parents, and they would tell my parents. Mom would put a stop to the trip before it started.

He looked through the telescope again, then asked, "Did you know there used to be another giant planet?"

"Another one?"

"Yeah, in addition to Jupiter, Saturn, Uranus, and Neptune, there was a fifth giant gas planet out there."

"What happened?"

"Jupiter knocked it out of orbit. One day it got too close, and Jupiter sent it hurtling out of the solar system."

I looked up at the sky. "Really rude, Jupiter." Then I asked Wendell, "So where is it now?"

"No one knows. Maybe another star pulled it onto a new orbit, and it's in that solar system now. Maybe it even has its own moons circling it. Or it's still out there on its own, flying past everything, on the same path Jupiter knocked it onto." He shrugged and looked away. "I know this is dumb, but sometimes I wonder about that planet. If I had a way of finding it, I'd go."

He hugged me then. I couldn't remember the last time we'd hugged, if ever. Maybe when we were little kids. I wanted to tell him that wasn't a dumb idea at all, but to do that I'd have to let go of him.

Wendell stepped back so I could see him again. "Good luck. Let me know when you find your whale."

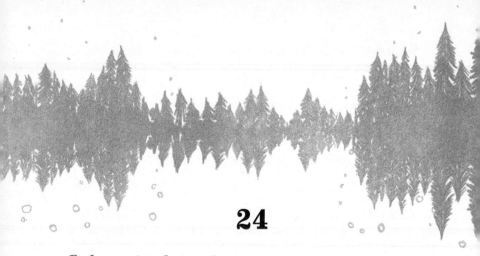

24

Each morning that week I tossed a few things into my backpack for the trip. Then after school I'd stop by Grandma's to move them to her closet. Her set of suitcases fit one inside the other like nesting dolls. We sat on the floor near her closet and added items to the small suitcase each day. The medium-size suitcase had been packed with Grandma's things since the day after she bought the tickets.

I'd been reading "What to Pack for Your Alaskan Vacation" articles so I'd know what to bring. People forget things when they travel to Alaska. They don't pack enough for the cold weather, thinking, *How bad can it be in the summer?* But it's a lot colder there, especially at night. Traveling on a boat is even worse, with all the wind. A good coat wasn't enough. You had to have gloves and a scarf and a hat and thick socks.

Of course I didn't have all those things, living in

Houston. In the corner of a dresser drawer was a pair of gloves I'd hardly worn. Even in winter I got by with my hands in my pockets. My sock supply was made up of those thin white ones that came six pairs to a package from Target. I'd packed extra pairs so I could double up. My gray sweatshirt had a hood. That would work for a hat. Plus, my hair was thick enough to protect me from the cold even if I went sledding across the Arctic tundra.

Before I left home that Saturday morning, I threw the last few things into my backpack. I gave an extra-long hug to each of my parents before leaving to meet Grandma. Dad asked if I was okay.

"Doing great," I answered, which was true. This was the most important thing I'd ever done. I was nervous, but mostly excited.

"Have fun at the beach," Mom told me. *"Call if you need anything."*

All I could do was nod for an answer before walking out the front door.

Maybe they would worry till I got back, but my leaving would be a relief in a way. No more explaining things for Dad, no more of him having to explain things to me. They'd have a kind of vacation too.

Tristan was in the driveway with Adam, looking

under the hood of Adam's truck. That was not unusual. The truck was always breaking down. Once, I leaned against it when Tristan started it up. It'd shaken like it was running on a lawn mower engine.

"*What's wrong with it?*" I asked. "*I know it's a long list, but what are you working on now?*"

"*It won't start,*" Tristan answered. "*Maybe needs a new battery.*"

"*Smells weird,*" I told him. "*Like a BBQ grill. Not in a good way.*"

"*Yeah, Adam dropped a cheeseburger last time he worked on the car. It's really stuck in there. So what do you think?*"

"*I think he shouldn't eat the rest of that cheeseburger if you get it out of there.*"

He grabbed a set of jumper cables from the bed of the truck. As soon as I lifted the plastic covers over the battery terminals for him, I saw the problem. I pointed at the caked-on corrosion. "*Clean those off and maybe it'll start.*"

Adam chuckled and rolled his eyes when Tristan told him what I'd said. I didn't miss the look of warning that Tristan gave him. "That's not a big deal," Adam said. "There's something else wrong."

On any other day I'd have grabbed the alternator

wire and carried it around in my backpack till Adam admitted I was right. But I'd be far away from there in a few hours, and Mom and Dad didn't need his dumb truck sitting in our driveway all week.

"Those battery wires don't even know they're connected to anything. Clean it with some baking soda or pour a Coke on it." After Tristan interpreted that, I asked him, *"Want to go get a breakfast taco? I have some time before I meet Grandma."*

He shook his head. *"I'll stay here and help fix this. We'll go tomorrow, okay?"*

"I'm telling you, pour a Coke on it and it'll start right up."

"Okay, we'll try that. Talk to you later."

I almost told him right then that I wouldn't be around tomorrow, or the next day, or a few days after that. But I just got on my bike and rode away.

There were plenty of Mexican restaurants around, and I'd been to all of them. The best breakfast tacos were at Carlos's Gas 'Em Up. One side was a convenience store, and the other was set up as a café. The owner, Carlos, and his whole family worked there.

I ordered a potato-egg-and-cheese taco, plus a small coffee—something more grown-up than my usual chocolate milk. After one bitter sip I tossed it in the trash can, then used a napkin to scrape the taste off my tongue. How could anyone drink that stuff? I went back to the counter for a chocolate milk.

As I sat there and ate, I looked around at the people who were reading the news or chatting with one another before work. I was dying to tell someone what I was about to do. I'd never held on to a secret this big, and it was bursting to get out. I went ahead and signed it right there to the whole room. No one would understand anyway, so it was a way of letting the secret out while still keeping it.

After finishing the last bite of my taco, I crumpled up the foil wrapper and signed, *"I should get going. Don't want to miss my flight. On my way to meet a whale."*

As I left the parking lot I saw Tristan and Adam driving up the road in Adam's truck. Obviously they'd fixed it and decided they had time for breakfast tacos after all. I almost went back. Maybe if they saw me, Tristan would've signed something like *"You were right."*

That was the only reason I thought about turning around. Not so I could say goodbye to him or anything.

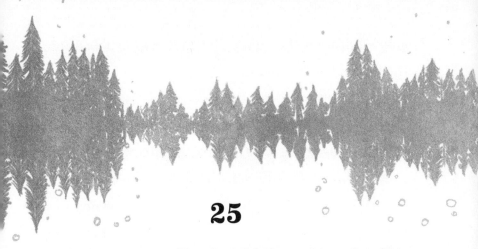

25

Even though it was still early, I pedaled as fast as I could to Grandma's. It'd be good to have a little extra time in case there were any glitches in our plan. Sometimes projects took longer than expected. Like the Philco radio. My stomach tightened with sadness. I missed resting my hand on it at night and feeling the vibrations from the radio programs. And then there was the fact I couldn't even touch the money I got from selling it.

I shook my head. Nothing I could do about the radio. Maybe I'd buy it back from Mr. Gunnar, unless someone else got to it first.

Grandma flung the door open as soon as I pressed the doorbell. She had to have been standing there waiting, or she'd leaped to the door as soon as the doorbell light flashed. She wore a flowery green dress and a long necklace with flower charms alternating in green and gold all around the chain. Her hair was brushed into the long silvery waterfall.

After opening up the suitcases on the floor of Grandma's closet, we checked our lists to make sure we weren't missing anything. The last thing we did before leaving the apartment was staple a blue tag from the cruise line around each suitcase handle. Seeing our names printed next to the cabin number on those tags made all our plans more real. We were doing this. Later that day we'd be rolling those bags onto the cruise ship.

When the elevator opened at the first floor of the building, we turned right, toward the side exit, instead of left, toward the front desk. The staff would have questions if they saw us heading to the front door with suitcases.

We loaded the luggage into the car without anyone stopping to talk to us.

"*Ready to go?*" Grandma asked after getting into the driver's seat.

"*Let's go find that whale,*" I answered.

Then I grabbed the armrest as the car peeled out of the parking lot and raced toward the freeway.

"*Slow down!*" I signed with only one hand so I could hang on with the other. Grandma didn't slow down; just changed lanes to fly past other cars. Maybe this was a bad idea. She hadn't driven much lately, and not on the freeway. If we got stopped by the police or wrecked the car, we wouldn't even make it to the airport.

Grandma laughed. *"I'm ready to start our adventure!"*

"Watch the road!" I didn't sign anything else after that, so I wouldn't give her a reason to take a hand off the wheel or her eyes off the freeway.

We made it to the airport alive. I released my grip on the armrest and slumped back to catch my breath when Grandma eased into a parking space.

After getting through the long security lines, we still had plenty of time to reach our gate. I wanted to take Grandma's hand and run onto the plane already, but we still had an hour before boarding.

We stopped at a coffee shop, where Grandma ordered a coffee and I got a lemonade iced tea. A little more grown-up than regular lemonade, but without the coffee taste. We shared a mammoth-size blueberry muffin. It was so delicious, I wondered if airport food was really that good or if everything tasted better because of the trip we were about to take. As we chatted I noticed Grandma's signing was faster, more excited than it had been lately. It matched the way she looked that day, as if the color was coming back to her signs too. She signed almost like she used to when Grandpa was around, and I wondered if she felt like he were with us. I had to eat without glancing down at my food so I wouldn't miss anything.

It didn't seem as if we'd been sitting at the coffee shop for long, but when I checked, I saw it was time to board.

We were almost in the last row of the flight since we'd bought the tickets so late. Grandma offered me the window seat, but I told her it was hers. I wanted her to enjoy the adventure as much as possible. Without her I wouldn't be there.

Under the settings on my phone, I found where to disable the GPS. I asked Grandma for hers so I could do the same thing. I didn't want my parents to worry about me, but I didn't want them tracking us down either.

"Hold on, I'll send your mom a message first." She handed me the phone after sending the text.

"What did you tell her?" I asked after turning off the GPS.

"I told her not to worry, that we're going farther than Surfside and will be gone a few days longer."

We smiled at each other and held hands as the

plane rolled down the runway and took off. This wasn't a game or a wish or a plan about a trip anymore. We were really going. Grandma was happier than I'd seen her for a long time.

This trip would kill two birds with one stone, as Dad would say. I'd meet the whale, and Grandma would be back to herself again.

After landing in San Francisco and picking up our luggage, we shuttled to the cruise terminal, where huge white ships sat in the water, waiting for passengers to board. I found ours and pointed it out to Grandma. The *Siren*. The ship that would sail me to Blue 55.

It was still too early to board, so we looked around for something to do. I'd been too excited until then to notice I was hungry, but my stomach was rumbling. *Like an airplane taking off.* I covered my stomach, even though Tristan wasn't there to hear it.

"*Lunch?*" I pointed to a seafood place with outdoor seating and a view of the ocean.

Grandma took my hand and led the way. The restaurant hostess seated us at a small table on a dock. We opened the menus and pointed to the same thing— a big platter with samples of every appetizer.

As I watched the waves next to us, I realized there was a smell I liked even better than old radio.

The ocean.

Checking in for the cruise was a lot like going through an airport again, only worse because we were so close to the ship. I wasn't going to breathe until we were safely aboard. Each part of the check-in process and every person in front of us was one more thing blocking my path to Blue 55.

After getting through the long line for the check-in counter, a woman with big blond hair gave us our cruise cards, which looked a lot like credit cards. They would be scanned when we bought something on board, and every time we got on or off the ship.

We thanked the woman at the counter, then moved over to yet another line to board the ship. The attendant at the end of that line held what looked like an alien gun, and we showed her our cards like the people in front of us had. She waved the gun to scan the bar codes on our cards before handing them back to us.

On our way to the metal ramp that led to the ship, a crew member stopped us for a picture. A sign on the wall in front of us read "Bon Voyage" next to a big picture of glaciers and blue water. Grandma put her arm around me, and we faced the camera, with the Alaskan backdrop behind us.

Finally it was really happening. Even though I was a few days away from meeting 55, I felt like I'd already accomplished something. At the end of the metal ramp that led to the ship, I stopped.

"*All right?*" Grandma asked. I squeezed her hand and smiled. Until then, the trip had been just a plan. Once we boarded the ship, it would be real. We'd sail away from land and try to find a whale. Grandma stood next to me like she understood that I needed to make the moment last. I wondered if she liked to put down a good book before turning to the last page too.

With one hand still holding Grandma's, I signed "*Ready*" with the other, then took a deep breath. Together we stepped from the metal ramp onto the plush carpet of the ship.

When we found our room on the fifth deck, a woman with dark brown skin, wearing black pants and a light blue shirt with gold buttons, smiled like it was the best news ever that we'd arrived. She shook our hands and said something to us. I guessed she was introducing herself. Her golden name tag read JOJO, CABIN STEWARD, GHANA. Grandma introduced us and let her know we were Deaf. Jojo took a business card from her pocket and wrote something on the back, then handed it to Grandma.

I leaned over to read it: *Customer relations can page me if you need anything.*

Jojo opened our door and handed us each a flyer with a map of the ship and a schedule for the rest of the day. She showed us around the cabin, which took two seconds since it was about the size of my bedroom at home.

After Jojo left, Grandma said she wanted to rest. Even after all the traveling and waiting in lines, I couldn't imagine sleeping any time soon. Grandma told me to go ahead and explore the ship.

First I found one of the swimming pools on the eighteenth deck. That wasn't even the highest point— there were two decks above that, with more pools and hot tubs and a game room. People gathered around the bars, holding bright pink and yellow drinks with little paper umbrellas perched on the edges of the glasses. The ship was like a floating city. It would be impossible to see everything, even with a week to explore. Still, I would try. I ran around like I had only a day to take it in.

A few more bars and restaurants were scattered

around the ship. On the same deck as customer service were gift shops, an internet café, and even a library.

A weird feeling that I couldn't place stirred in my stomach. I was restless, as if I were forgetting something. Maybe I'd been so busy working on my plan to meet 55, and there wasn't anything left to do but wait.

At the safety drill that afternoon, the crew herded everyone from our deck into one of the bars. They showed us how to put on life jackets and where the lifeboats were so if the ship hit an iceberg, we wouldn't end up like the passengers on the *Titanic*.

Afterward we stood on the deck and looked out at the water we'd be sailing across soon. The color wasn't the same as what I was used to. The water in the Gulf Coast always looked a little muddy. This was much bluer. Sea lions lounged on the wooden docks of the harbor.

More people with their fruity umbrella drinks mingled around us. The railing vibrated against my hands, and I looked around to see what was making noise. People around us clapped, with their mouths opened like they were laughing and cheering.

Grandma looked up and covered her ear that wore a hearing aid.

"*What is that?*" I asked.

"Foghorn." She lowered her hand to add, *"That means it's time to leave."*

The ship lurched as it pulled away from the dock. If anyone back home figured out where to look for Grandma and me, well ... they'd find that ship had sailed.

26

I hadn't seen any kids on the ship, which wasn't a surprise since school was still going on. But that evening at the "welcome aboard" party, a girl across the pool waved to me. She looked about my age and had straight black hair, light brown skin, and the kind of glasses I'd wear if I needed them—black frames that made you look smart. I waved back. It seemed like she might come talk to me. I was there for Blue 55, but I couldn't get to him any faster than the ship would go. Maybe it'd be nice to have someone else to talk to while I was on board. Most passengers looked older than Grandma.

Grandma tapped my shoulder. *"Dinner?"* She downed the last of her drink, then stuck the paper umbrella behind her ear. I nodded and looked back at the girl, then waved again as we left the deck. I'd look for her later.

Each table in the dining room was covered with a

white cloth and had a silver vase of flowers. Some people sat at big round tables; others sat at booths or tables for four. Grandma and I had our own table by a window. The waiter—CONSTANTIN, ROMANIA—unfurled the cloth napkins and placed them in our laps.

It was the nicest restaurant I'd ever been to. When I opened the menu, I got really worried.

"There aren't any prices," I signed to Grandma.

"Get whatever you want," she answered. *"It's all included in the price of the cruise."*

Of course. It seemed so much like a real restaurant that I'd forgotten we were on a ship.

"It's okay," she added. She could probably tell I was embarrassed. *"At some restaurants on board, you do pay at the end, but not in the dining rooms and the buffet."* She looked over the menu and said, *"Let's get two different things and share."*

When Constantin returned with a basket of rolls and a butter dish, Grandma told him she'd like the tilapia with rice and steamed vegetables. She signed at the same time she was talking to him so I'd know what she was ordering. Then Constantin turned to me, and I pointed to the salmon with mashed potatoes. He said something else, then flipped the menu over when

I didn't understand him. The dessert page. Everything looked so good, even the things I'd never heard of. Grandma signed, *"I'll get the cheesecake. Which one do you want?"*

I wanted to say *"One of each,"* but decided on the crème brûlée. *"Not sure what it is, but I'll find out."*

Grandma laughed and said *"Good choice"* as I pointed it out to Constantin.

It was nice to see Grandma laugh. I didn't expect her to ever stop missing Grandpa, but maybe this trip would help her get back to her normal self again. Ever since we'd started the planning, it seemed like that drizzly November in her was looking brighter.

The water outside the window looked flat and smooth, except for the white-capped wake the ship made as it sped through the ocean.

Grandma touched my shoulder and signed, *"Look!"*

I turned to see what had caught her attention. The dark gray triangles sticking out of the water reminded me of sharks' fins. But then the animals leaped in arches out of the water together, five of them diving down into the waves and then jumping back up again.

"Dolphins!"

Grandma clapped her hands. *"Yes! Looks like they're*

racing the boat." The pod of dolphins jumped and dived together next to the ship. It felt like a good sign, seeing them as our journey started.

I wondered if Grandma wished that Grandpa were there, watching the dolphins with her. They were supposed to take this cruise together. I wanted to ask her about him, but thinking of him might make her sad. She probably thought about him all the time, though. So maybe it wouldn't hurt to mention him.

"What was your favorite cruise?" I asked her after Constantin brought our plates.

She handed me a forkful of tilapia. *"Hard to choose. I liked them all. After so much time I can't remember which beach was which. But my favorite memory was when we found the karaoke bar."*

"Really?" Of all the entertainment they'd seen on their travels, watching people sing at a karaoke machine couldn't have been the most interesting.

"Yes. I think it was on our cruise to Jamaica. We were wandering the ship at night and felt loud music coming from one of the bars." Grandma covered her ear like she had when the foghorn sounded. Then both hands bounced and fluttered in front of her, showing me how the thumping bass of the music trembled the floor.

"The Calypso, the bar was called. We stopped in to get a

drink and see what was going on. That was the first time we saw a karaoke machine. We sat and watched for a few minutes, then put our names on the list to take a turn ourselves."

"You and Grandpa? At the karaoke machine?"

"Yes. The words to the songs were right there on the screen. That was really for the people who were singing, but it allowed us to enjoy the lyrics, too, instead of just watching people sing."

"So what did you do when it was your turn?"

"We signed one of our favorite songs! When we flipped through the big book of all the songs the club could play, we found one from a musical we had interpreted in college."

"And you got up and did the song together?" As hard as I tried, I couldn't imagine my grandparents standing in front of a crowd in a karaoke bar.

"We did! And Grandpa got the crowd to sing along as we signed the lyrics. He was always good at bringing other people in. You're like him in that way—able to communicate with people you don't know. I'm always in my own head too much to know what to say to other people."

Grandma must have been thinking about someone else. I didn't ask her what she meant because she looked so happy talking about Grandpa I didn't want to interrupt the memory.

"And when the song was over, we got a standing

ovation! We started to go back to our table, but the next couple asked if we'd sign while they sang. We kept it going the rest of the night. We didn't know many of the songs, but we did what we could on the spot with the lyrics in front of us." She shrugged. "And so what if we did mess up? No one would know."

I couldn't believe I hadn't heard that story before. I'd have to ask Mom about it when I got home. Maybe she didn't know all that either. I found myself wondering then what my parents were thinking. After all the planning I'd done, I was there on the ship, right where I was supposed to be. At the same time, I wanted to be at home with my family at the dinner table, even if I didn't always catch everything they talked about. They must have been worried about us by now. Or angry. Maybe both. But if I called to tell them we were okay, I'd end up explaining more than I wanted to. "Let the cat out of the bag" was another expression I'd never understood. What does that have to do with telling a secret? And why would a cat be in a bag anyway?

I didn't realize I was smiling until Grandma brushed two fingertips along the end of her nose and then shrugged to ask, "What's so funny?"

"Just thinking about Dad," I answered. "Some of the things he says . . ."

"Like when he says 'Let's hit the road' and looks like he's punching a street?"

"Yeah, that." When Dad showed me that humpback whale record he used to listen to, I should have shown him the website with all the different whale songs. Maybe he'd like to hear them again. I wondered when he'd stopped listening to them.

Grandma and I were both too full to finish our dinners, but we magically found more room when Constantin set our desserts in front of us. I still wasn't sure what crème brûlée was made of, other than sugar and some sort of cream. Whatever it was, it was my new favorite food.

When Constantin returned to clear our plates, he showed me a note that read *How do you sign "beautiful"?* It's a little hard for a new person to sign, but he practiced it a couple of times and did okay.

As we got up to leave, he signed to Grandma, *"Goodbye, Beautiful."*

I couldn't believe it. Grandma was actually blushing.

When we got back to the room, the clear plastic holder next to our door held two packets. I gave one to Grandma and flipped through the other as I sat on the edge of the bed.

I waved to get Grandma's attention, then when she looked up, I asked, *"What do you want to do tomorrow?"*

She turned a page of the schedule. *"I don't know. Try my luck at the casino, maybe."*

One thing caught my eye as I scanned the next day's events. An Alaskan wildlife presentation by Sura Kilabuk, the naturalist aboard the ship. Alaskan wildlife had to include whales. It'd be a few days before we got to the sanctuary, but until then I could learn more about Blue 55. Maybe Sura knew about him. Since Grandma didn't pay for Wi-Fi access, I wouldn't be able to check online to see where he was while we were at sea. I'd feel better if I at least knew which way to look.

27

He called out to anyone, to no one. Then stopped to listen. Noises filled the sea around him. Dolphins chattered as they leaped in arcs above the surface. Waves swelled and crashed. Water bubbles popped when a school of fish scrambled away. The low songs of whales traveled through the ocean. A sea full of sounds, with none for him.

He reached for those songs he couldn't sing, trying to grab a call when a wave of sound trembled the water.

If only he could catch it, he'd keep it with him until the sound became a part of him. Then he would answer back and make the tremor of his song float through the water like theirs, and they would know him and answer.

Was there anything out in the ocean like himself? He kept calling just in case his someone was there.

28

I've had breakfast buffets before, but nothing like what was on the ship. It was more like every breakfast buffet from every restaurant I'd ever been in, all shoved into one place. It'd be impossible to try everything. I'd never had French toast and waffles and pancakes in the same meal. We'd picked a good cruise, even though there hadn't been many choices left.

Grandma went to lie by the pool and look out at the ocean while I went to the wildlife lecture. I found my way to a big theater with hundreds of cushy red seats and a stage. It was too early for the presentation, so just a few people were scattered around the theater.

Sitting in the middle of the front row was the girl I'd seen by the pool the evening before. Maybe she liked whales too. I pulled my notepad and pen from my pocket as I took the seat next to her.

Two people stood on stage near the podium, fiddling

with the microphones and getting the slideshow ready. The one holding the microphone had the same straight black hair and light brown skin as the girl next to me.

I'm Iris. I'm Deaf, I wrote on the notepad.

I laughed when I read what she wrote back. *I'm Bennie. Not Deaf.* Good, so she wasn't afraid of me.

You like whales? I asked her. *Or other animals?*

Most animals. Especially sharks. I'm going to be a shark biologist.

Working with sharks? Maybe this girl wasn't afraid of anything.

I get to come here with my mom every summer when she's working on the ship, she added to the note.

I pointed to the woman at the podium, and Bennie nodded.

BRB, she wrote. At the front of the stage, she waved her mom over. Sura leaned over to talk to her and looked in my direction when Bennie pointed. Sura returned to the computer on the podium while Bennie ran back to her seat next to me.

People in the audience settled into their seats and turned toward the stage when Sura talked into the microphone. Since we were so close to the front of the theater, I could see her mouth and catch some of what she said. It seemed like Sura was looking at me while she talked, and she held the microphone low enough that it didn't hide her mouth. Bennie must have told her I was Deaf. That morning Grandma said that she should have requested sign language interpreters for us, but everything happened so fast that she didn't think of it until we left. I hadn't thought of it at all, since I didn't know interpreters ever worked on cruises.

Soon the lights dimmed for the PowerPoint presentation. A spotlight stayed on Sura as she narrated over the slideshow, but with all the pictures and video clips and text on the screen, I could follow along without watching her.

Alaska sure had a lot of wildlife. I thought we'd never get to the whales. It was interesting stuff, I had to admit. Black bears weren't as scary as I'd thought. They pretty much leave you alone. You just have to stay out of their way and make some noise when you're in their area so you won't startle them once they see you. Grizzly bears are a different story. You wouldn't want to come face to face with them whether or not they were expecting you.

After looking at pictures of bald eagles, mountain goats, seals, and sea lions, I nudged Bennie and wrote on the notepad: *Any whales?*

Whales are last, she answered.

Maybe that was Sura's way of getting everyone to stick around for the whole talk, saving the most interesting animal for last.

Finally we got to the whale part of the presentation.

On a slide with the heading "Bubble Net Feeding," Sura showed a pod of humpback whales feeding on a bunch of fish. She clicked over to a video titled "Whale Watchers Capture Bubble Net Feeding in Action."

The humpback pod worked as a team to hunt for their food. The whales zoomed in on a school of small fish. They circled and circled to drive the fish into a tighter and tighter group. Once all the fish were in a tight bundle, one whale blew bubbles from his blowhole while the rest continued to circle. That's why it was called bubble net feeding: the fish wouldn't swim through the bubbles, so it kept them in place like a net would. Then the loudest whale dove below the school of fish and bellowed a feeding call. The bellowing drove the fish into a tighter ball and up to the surface as they tried to escape the sound.

I wondered how the whales decided who was the loudest or who was the best bubbler. Did they have tryouts or something? I knew that whales were smart, from everything I'd read, but that took some serious planning. Maybe Sura would know. At the end of the presentation, I asked Bennie if she could introduce me. She nodded and pointed out to the hallway.

Sura sat behind a table stacked with books, and people were already lining up to talk to her. She signed the books for passengers who bought them. Bennie and I chatted back and forth using the notepad, with some gesturing and pointing thrown in. I got that she and her mom were from northern Canada, which was really cold.

The woman in line ahead of us was never going to stop talking. I shifted from one foot to the other while we waited for her to ask her thousand questions about every species of animal in Alaska or whatever she was doing. Finally she moved on, and Bennie introduced me to her mom. Sura held her hand out and said, "Nice to meet you." After shaking her hand, I showed her the question I'd written on the paper. *The bubble net feeding. How'd they figure that out?*

She wrote down an answer, then slid the paper over to me.

We're not sure. Amazing, aren't they?

Okay, yes, but what kind of answer was that?

But I want to know how they communicate, I wrote. *How'd they come up with that plan for catching fish?*

I'd worked with radios enough to know how each

part communicates with the next. Shouldn't scientists who study whales know all about how they talk to one another?

That's one fun thing about science, Sura wrote. *The wondering. If we knew all the answers, there wouldn't be anything to search for.*

Well, that didn't sound like much fun to me, leaving a bunch of questions unanswered.

Bennie said something to her mom, and Sura's answer looked like "Great idea!"

She turned a page in the notepad and wrote, *Tomorrow I'll be announcing whale sightings from the bridge. You're welcome to join us there if you'd like. You'll get the best views.*

Where is that? I wrote. When I explored the ship, I hadn't seen anything that looked like a bridge.

Deck eight. Bennie can show you.

That did sound good—getting the chance to see whales in the wild. Maybe Grandma would like that too.

What time?

I'll be up there by 5 a.m. You know what they say: the early bird gets the whale. No, I didn't know anyone who said that. Not even my dad.

Bennie took the notepad and wrote, *Meet for breakfast at 6?*

Okay, I'll ask my grandma.

Sura wrote, *She's welcome to come too.*

Grandma wouldn't want to wake up that early, but I'd ask anyway. I wasn't a morning person either, but if that was when the whales got up, I would too.

Do you know Blue 55? I asked Sura. *I'm wondering where he's swimming now.*

I was ready to tell her all about 55 and his song if she didn't know who he was, but she smiled and pulled her phone from her pocket. A blue icon on the phone screen was labeled "Track 55." The map that came up when she opened the app showed a black dotted line with a blinking blue dot at the end. It looked kind of like the map I'd seen online.

That's him? I wrote.

Yes. This app shows where his song was last picked up, but it's been a while since anyone's heard him. Sura zoomed in on the map, then pointed behind us and to the right. *Out that way, last anyone knew.*

After thanking Sura and Bennie and telling them goodbye, I took the elevator up to the top deck and stood at the railing. I looked in the direction Sura had pointed and felt closer to Blue 55.

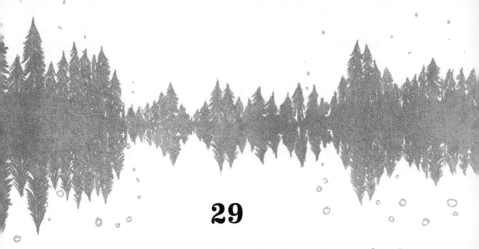

29

Bennie waited for me outside the buffet entrance. I'd told Grandma the night before that she was invited to come with me to watch for whales from the bridge, but when I mentioned the time, she flopped over in bed like just the thought of waking up so early was enough to knock her out. *"I'll wait for whales that wake up at a more reasonable hour."*

Bennie led me through the dining area, and I shrugged as a way of asking "Where are we going?" She pointed toward the back of the room and gave a thumbs-up.

I'd felt like I was getting used to the ship, but it was full of surprises. Bennie led me past the lines of people, through one dining area to another, almost to the back of the deck, where there was another buffet line. It served the exact same stuff as the first one, but there wasn't a long wait. Most people stopped at the first food line they saw, like I had.

We took our salmon eggs Benedict and banana waffles to an outdoor table, with a view of the ocean around us. I set my notepad and pen between us, and Bennie handed me a rolled-up navy-blue scarf from her coat pocket.

I pointed to myself and mouthed, *For me?*

She nodded and pointed to me too, then rubbed her arms and pretended to shiver. True, I had been cold, but I didn't know it was that obvious. Even with my coat zipped all the way up last night, the wind chilled my neck and upper chest.

"Thanks," I signed. I tied the scarf around my neck, and Bennie stood up to show me how to tuck it under the collar of my coat. Big difference.

She wrote on the notepad, *I thought you might want to borrow a scarf since it didn't seem like you had one. You're out of school already?*

Bennie had told me the night before that her parents homeschooled her, then boat-schooled her when her mom worked on cruise ships. I thought about making up something to tell her why I was there but realized I didn't mind telling her the real story. Even though we'd just met, I felt like I'd known her for a long time.

I shook my head. *School's still going on. I had to come now because I want to meet Blue 55.*

Bennie's eyebrows rose, and her mouth dropped open as she read the note. "You're going to meet him? I mean, sorry, I forgot—"

I waved her off as she reached for the pen, since I understood what she'd said. It felt good to share my plan with someone who was as excited about the whale as I was.

I hope so, I wrote. *He's supposed to be in Appleton around the time we get there.* I hesitated before telling her about the song. She might think it was a dumb idea. But she knew more about whales than I did. Better to find out now if something was wrong with my plan. If she told me it wouldn't work out, I didn't know what I'd do.

I made a song for him. The sanctuary workers will play it from the boat when they go out to tag him. I looked down at my plate as I slid the notepad to her, then glanced up to see her expression.

She smiled while she scribbled on the page. *Can I hear it later?*

Sure. I took the last bite of my waffle and smiled back at her. Bennie knew more about whales than I did, and she liked my plan. Maybe it really would work.

After breakfast Bennie led me to the bridge of the

ship, which as it turned out was not like a bridge at all, so I wasn't sure how it had gotten that name. It was a giant room that took up the middle of deck eight. Floor-to-ceiling windows wrapped around the room, giving us a view in all directions. A long wooden counter topped with a dashboard of screens stretched across the bridge. So many dials, knobs, buttons, and joysticks filled the counter, I couldn't imagine how anyone ever learned what they were all for. A few overhead screens showed a radar, views of the ship, a map of our route, and rows of numbers that must have meant something to someone. A man dressed in black pants and a white shirt with gold stripes on the sleeves stood at the front of the bridge, looking out. I figured he was the captain. A couple of other crew members sat in black leather chairs at the controls.

For a few minutes we stood at our places near the front windows while Sura made announcements into a microphone. Nothing but still waters stretched out ahead of us. Maybe it was the wrong day to look for whales. I turned when Sura pointed to our right. At first I didn't see anything. Then a plume of spray shot into the air. Bennie glanced at me and motioned like she was writing with an invisible pen.

Humpbacks, she wrote after I handed her my notepad. I looked out at the water again. Even though Sura had binoculars, I didn't know how she could tell what kinds of whales were out there from so far away. Closer to the ship, a whale shot up out of the water, then crashed down with a giant splash. It almost didn't seem real. The whale was about the size of a school bus, and there he was flying out of the ocean. I turned to Bennie to ask, *Did that really happen?* The wonder on her face answered my question. She must have seen whales a thousand times, but she still looked thrilled at the sight of them.

Another whale breached, then left behind a wall of splashing water after it sank beneath the surface again. Seeing them in real life was nothing like looking at pictures or videos. I ran to the windows closest to the whale who had just leaped up from the water. Bennie tapped my shoulder and pointed to the other side of the ship. I looked in time to see another whale crashing down onto the ocean's surface.

I'd have to try to describe all this to Dad. I hoped I'd be able to get across how beautiful they were. These were the whales he listened to so much on that old record. The humpbacks, the symphony players.

After a while I got better at catching sight of the spray from the whales' blowholes, so I knew where they were. Sura estimated we were surrounded by about fifty whales. I wondered if Blue 55 ever swam with other whales, even though they didn't speak the same language. Andi had said he'd swim toward other whales, but then he'd go back to swimming alone again. Maybe he swam *near* those other whales but not really *with* them. Kind of like how I was at school.

When Bennie let me know that her mom was wrapping up the whale watch announcements for the morning, I looked at the time and realized we'd been on the bridge for more than two hours already. Hadn't I just gotten there?

Before we left I wrote a note for Sura. *How'd you know they were humpbacks from so far away?*

She waved me over to a table and pulled out a chair for me. From her messenger bag she removed a folder and flipped through some papers until she found the one she was looking for. The paper had a bunch of pictures of blow spouts from whales. The top of the page had the heading "There She Blows!"

Like in Moby-Dick, I wrote. Captain Ahab said that when he saw a spout from the white whale. I remembered some of the book from a kids' edition that Grandma had given me. I'd tried to finish it a few times because I wanted to find out if the whale got away from the people who were hunting him, but I always fell asleep before I got to the end.

Sura nodded and wrote, *Each kind of whale has its own spout shape. If I spot them before the wind blows away the spray, I can identify what kind it is.* She pointed to the picture of a humpback. The water that shot up from the whale's blowhole was shaped like an upside-down teardrop. Some other whales blew out water in almost the same shape, but in a taller, thinner teardrop than the humpback's. Gray and right whales blew double spouts of water in the shape of a heart.

Sura turned to another page in her notebook, which showed pictures of whale flukes. Those were all different shapes, too. If she was close enough to see a whale's tail, she'd know what kind of whale it belonged to.

On the back of the paper, I wrote, *What about Blue 55?* and slid it over to Sura.

At the bottom of the page, she drew a quick sketch. Blue 55 had a fin on his back like a fin whale, and the tail of a blue whale. Another way he was different from any other.

30

It would be easier if he could forget the others he'd sung to. But the memory of a whale is long and deep. A whale who swims in the ocean for a century still remembers the first whales he knew. Just as strongly, he remembers those he never knew, the ones who drifted past.

He dove below a wave. The deeper he swam, the more the water resisted, pushed him back up where he didn't want to be. At the ocean's surface the sunlight illuminated the whale families he couldn't belong to.

He pushed back, swimming harder, until the dark swallowed him. The depths were emptier, darker, quieter. Yet less lonely, because there was no one to answer his calls with silence.

What was a whale without a pod? What was a whale without a whale song?

He didn't try to create a song by sending air flowing through his body. He kept his breath still.

Air and space did not make music.

Air was only air.

Space was nothing more than space.

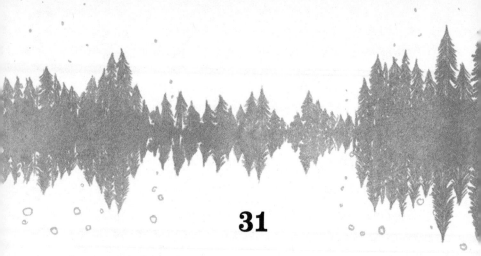

31

It was our third day on the ship already, but it felt like I'd just left home. At the same time the days somehow passed slowly. At lunch I'd think of a conversation I'd had that morning, and it felt like it had happened days ago. It wasn't going by slowly in a bad way. Not dragging like on a school day where you'd swear someone had glued the hands of the clock into place. Each night I wasn't ready for the day to end, even though it seemed it had started so long ago. I almost forgot why I was on the ship—to meet Blue 55. Almost. Each day on the ship brought me closer to him.

I didn't want to spend the day in the cabin, but I wasn't going to do anything until my stomach settled down. It churned every time I sat up. When Jojo came by to clean the room, I told her I wasn't feeling well.

She picked up a notepad from the nightstand and wrote, *Back in a minute*. When she returned she propped the door open and handed me a cold can of pineapple juice.

I slid the notepad across the nightstand while she made Grandma's bed. *Thanks. Guess I'm seasick.*

She took the pen from me and added, *Usually people don't get seasick when the sailing is this smooth.*

True, the boat hadn't been rocking at all. Whenever I looked out into the ocean, there was hardly a wave. I didn't know another explanation for how I felt, though.

Jojo handed me a new page she'd written on. *I haven't seen my family for six months. Sometimes I miss them so much I feel sick. Maybe you're homesick?*

I'd always thought "homesick" meant you just missed being away from home and wanted to go back. I never knew it could make you actually feel sick. Maybe that was what was wrong with me. It wasn't just that I missed home. Mixed in with that was everything I was worried about, like how mad my parents must be and whether or not I'd get to meet Blue 55. What if the sick feeling was my body trying to tell me that I shouldn't be here on this ship? If my plan didn't work, Blue 55 would swim through the ocean as lonely as always, and I'd go back home to face the trouble I was in, all for nothing.

The feeling was much worse than the emptiness

I felt in my stomach when I had to leave a radio sitting broken on the shelf. It was like an emptiness that was never going to go away.

Of course I couldn't tell Jojo any of that. I smiled and thanked her again for the juice.

When I caught up with Bennie later, she pulled a notebook from her pocket. She'd started carrying one like I did, to write messages to me. She was picking up a little sign language, too, so we communicated more and more with signs. She didn't pretend to know more than she did, and she didn't mind when I corrected her. She even laughed at her own mistakes, like when she signed *"bathroom"* instead of *"Tuesday."* Some signs were pretty close, but just moving the hand the wrong way made a big difference in meaning.

"Are you and your grandma getting off the ship in Juneau?" she asked.

"Yeah. Not sure what we'll do." That day would be the ship's first port stop. Some people would spend the day in Juneau and go sightseeing or on a small boat for a whale watch. We'd seen so many whales from the ship, but most passengers didn't have the view from the bridge like Bennie and I had.

"Think I'll look for someplace with internet so I can check in with my parents." I'd been thinking I should

send a message to my family. They had to be worried, even though Grandma said she was updating Mom to let her know we were okay. When I asked her what Mom had said, she just waved me off and told me, *"She'll get over it."*

Use the internet café here on the ship, Bennie wrote. *I can log you on as our guest.*

You can? Like for free? I didn't think Grandma would want to pay for internet time, but I hadn't thought about asking Bennie to help me get online.

Sure, I'll show you how.

That offer was too good to turn down. *Okay, great! Do you have something you can do too? I don't want you to be bored while I check email and stuff.*

Yeah, I'll watch shark videos.

The café was like a coffee shop, with a counter where people could order drinks and snacks. Some people sat at tables and chairs with their laptops. Mounted along each wall was a narrow table with desktop computers. Bennie pointed to the cups of gelato behind a glass case near the counter and gave me a thumbs-up. After we each got a dish—chocolate mint for her, red velvet for me—I sat at a computer near a window, all the way to the right. Starboard, I should say. Bennie had taught me some ship vocabulary. The right side of the ship was the starboard side, and the left was the port. The front was the bow, the back the stern. But some signs on the walls pointed out the fore and aft parts of the ship so I wasn't sure what the differences were.

Bennie pulled up a chair next to me and showed me how to log into the ship's Wi-Fi, then opened the computer's notepad. *The cruise line gives us some guest accounts, like for when my dad or a friend is visiting. You can use that login while you're here.*

Wow, thanks! First I checked on Blue 55. The map on the sanctuary's website showed a dotted line, not the solid one I'd hoped to see. A guess of where he was. He still wasn't singing.

I hadn't noticed that Bennie was looking at the map too until she squeezed my hand. She turned her screen so I could see it, and typed, *Sometimes I don't feel like talking to anyone either. Maybe he's like that.*

Since no one ever answered him back, I couldn't blame Blue 55 if he quit singing forever. I wished I could tell him how close I was and that I had a song for him. He couldn't give up just yet.

Bennie tapped my arm and signed, *"Song?"*

Right, I'd told her I'd play Blue 55's song for her. I brought up the sound file from my email, then hit play.

Bennie's mouth dropped open like she couldn't

believe what she was hearing. She turned to a man across the room and said sorry, then hit the volume down button on the keyboard.

She pointed at me like she was asking "You did this?"

I laughed at her surprise. *"Yes."*

"How?"

I signed *"school,"* then pretended I was playing each instrument one by one. *"And ..."* I opened the tuner app on my phone, then turned the wheel to "Tuba" and invited Bennie to tap some of the notes. The hertz readout in the corner showed her how close the notes were to fifty-five hertz.

"Cool!" Bennie signed. After trying out a few more instruments on the tuner, she clicked to a screen I hadn't used before and said something into the phone. A line graph rose and fell as she talked. This screen had a hertz readout too, showing the frequency of Bennie's voice. Way too high for the whale—almost two hundred hertz—but it was interesting to see. She held the phone in front of me, inviting me to talk into it.

"Me?"

"Try it."

I glanced around to see if anyone else was looking at us, then leaned toward the phone. I'd do something quiet. The wavy blue line appeared on the graph when I hummed and then skipped higher when I giggled. Bennie and I took turns humming into the phone to see what the graph and hertz readout would do. If I hummed deeply enough to feel the vibrations in my chest, I could make the frequency lower. Interesting, but it still wasn't going to get anywhere near fifty-five hertz, no matter what I did.

That must be what it was like for Blue 55. He knew what sound he needed to make but just couldn't do it. I closed the app and typed a message to Bennie: *I wish I could make a sound like his. I'd add it to the song.*

Maybe that was what was bothering me about the song I'd made—all the notes that played at his frequency were made with instruments. Even though I'd added the sounds of other animals to it, there wasn't a living thing that sounded like him. Only Blue 55 himself.

Bennie signed *"Wait,"* then pulled her own phone from her pocket. She opened an app that showed a picture of a microphone in the center of the screen and a sliding bar marked "Lower" and "Higher" on either side.

Bennie touched the microphone, then talked into the phone. She pointed to my phone and drew a check mark in the air, asking me to check what she'd just recorded. I opened the tuner app and held the phones side by side while Bennie's recording played. One hundred hertz. A lot lower than her real voice.

The graph on my phone bounced as I laughed. *"Can you make it lower?"*

Bennie scrolled the bar on her voice modulator app until the readout on my screen told us we'd hit the magic number. Fifty-five. She held the phone toward me again and hit the record button. I hummed at the phone, then we adjusted the recording until it would sound like something Blue 55 might recognize. Bennie said she'd email the sound files to me so I could add them to the song. I wasn't sure how I'd do that without my computer software, but I searched on my phone for audio editing apps and found a free one that looked good. I'd be able to load the song onto it and then slide in the files from Bennie.

I slid the keyboard back to me and typed, *Can you show me that tracker your mom had for Blue 55?*

She held her hand out, then added the tracker for me after I gave her my phone. I'd be able to check on 55's progress without having to get on a computer.

Time to check email. I held my breath as I signed in. Just as I thought, the screen was full of unread messages. Besides my parents and Tristan, Wendell had emailed me. I scrolled down to the first one, sent the day I left.

> Let me know when you get where you're going.

And two days later:

> Did you get there? Where are you going to look for the whale? I'm getting worried.

For me the days were flying by, but they had to be crawling for everyone back home. I couldn't believe I hadn't thought of that. I was almost too embarrassed to answer Wendell.

> Wendell,
>   Sorry I didn't get in touch before, but I haven't had internet service. I'm okay. After I find the whale, I'll tell you all about him.

The messages from my family were about the same, wanting me to let them know where I was and if I was all right. Mom added:

Grandma says you'll be gone a few days. Is that true? How are you going to make up all the work you're missing at school? I'll go by there and pick up your books, but I'd like to know what to tell them.

Don't worry about being in trouble. I'm sure this was your grandmother's idea. It's the kind of thing she'd do.

I could leave it at that and let Grandma take the blame. Maybe I wouldn't be grounded for life after we got back.

Mom,

Everything's okay. I'll catch up on my work when I get back. Please don't worry. I'm having a great time with Grandma. Yes, it'll be a few days before we get back. Sorry for taking off like we did without telling you first.

I guess it's the kind of thing I'd do too, because it wasn't Grandma's idea. Please don't be mad at her.

Love,

Iris

Houses and buildings added to the landscape of mountains and snow as we closed in on Juneau. Grandma would be ready to get off the ship. That morning she said she'd meet me back in our cabin so we could go into town together.

The cabin was empty when I got back. I found Jojo in the hall and asked if she'd seen Grandma. She didn't know where she was either.

Grandma wouldn't leave the ship without me. Would she? I sat on the edge of the bed to wait.

She'd been having so much fun on the cruise. This is what we'd all been wanting her to do at Oak Manor—join in on the activities and make some friends. But that wasn't the point of this trip. We were there to meet Blue 55.

Thinking of Oak Manor reminded me of why Grandma was living there. Maybe Mom was right about Grandma needing people to look out for her. I was having fun too, but I was ready to be on land again for a few hours. And I wouldn't take off somewhere and forget Grandma.

Just before I gave up to go look for her, the cabin door opened, and in walked Grandma.

"Ready to go?" she asked.

"Yeah, I'm ready. Where were you?"

"Origami class." She held up a red paper swan. Its long neck moved back and forth, and the wings flapped when she pulled gently on the swan's tail.

"You did that in your class?"

"Yes, with just one square of paper." Grandma showed me how she'd folded the square again and again to create the swan. "And I made something for you." She pulled another folded paper shape out of her purse and placed it into my hand. A blue whale.

"Like it?" she asked.

"You made this for me?" I moved a delicate fin up and down with my fingertip.

"With some help. I stayed after class to ask the teacher how to make a whale."

I couldn't let on I'd been annoyed with her or that I'd worried she'd left me. Even though Grandma had been at her own class and meeting other people, she was thinking of me. And the whale. She didn't forget the reason we were there.

I set the whale on the nightstand and thought about Grandpa's poems. Paper wasn't always flat. Sometimes it was folded into a shape that used the space around and above and below it to tell a story.

A brochure from our cabin showed what there was

to do and see in Juneau. One page pictured trails that were easy to walk.

"Maybe a hike?" I suggested.

"I have another plan," Grandma answered.

"Another plan?" I hadn't noticed her looking at the Juneau information.

She pulled two tickets from her purse and handed one to me. Printed in black letters across the ticket were the words "Glacier Shuttle, All-Day Pass."

"We'll see the glaciers up close?"

"And touch them."

Like Grandpa wanted to do.

We made our way to the shuttle stop near the cruise ship terminal and boarded along with a few other people who'd gathered at the corner. The driver waited until the bus was almost full before pulling away from the curb.

Near the end of the twenty-minute ride, the shuttle left the paved road and drove through bumpy tree-lined trails. The driver pulled up to a narrower trail, and we got out to follow wooden signs the rest of the way to the glaciers. I wanted to run up the path, but I walked slowly enough to keep pace with Grandma. Bennie's blue scarf tucked under my coat collar shielded my neck from the cold air. I'd have to thank her again for letting me borrow it.

We stopped to read a sign with a picture of a U-shape valley, covered with blue-and-white ice. The description beneath the picture said that glaciers carved the mountains there. For millions of years, the heavy ice crawled over the mountains like a slow bulldozer, knocking aside dirt and rocks as it reshaped the mountainside.

I looked ahead of us at the glaciers, trying to imagine them carving out the curves between mountain peaks. I'd always signed *"valley"* with my hands moving down to a V shape, but maybe that wasn't always right. So the glaciers would reshape my sign, too. From now on, whenever I described to anyone what the valleys here looked like, I'd soften the sign into more of a U shape.

After a few minutes we were close enough to touch the glassy, ice-covered mountains. We'd sailed by some glaciers on the way, but the view from the ship didn't show the reflections of blue in the ice. Other colors, too, ones I didn't have names for. Maybe they didn't have names because they didn't exist anywhere but in glaciers. Ignoring the cold, I removed a glove to run my hand along the ice. We were there to touch a glacier, and touching it with a glove probably wouldn't count. The wall of ice was smooth, but not flat like I'd thought it would be. Like frozen waves instead of the flat sheets they looked to be from a distance. In some areas the ice was so thick, it seemed the mountain was made of ice. Then, just a few feet away, brown rock showed through a hazy ice window.

This was the same stuff I got out of the freezer at home for my water glass, but it was so much more than that. This frozen water was powerful enough to carve mountains. It sculpted the landscape here, as if it decided there would be a peak, over there would be a valley, over there a ribbon of ice running down the mountain. Sure, I'd learned about glaciers in school, but it was kind of like the breaching humpbacks— seeing them up close made them more real.

A man who looked like a park ranger, dressed all in brown, talked to some of the people who'd been on our shuttle. I wondered how he could hear anything through the furry flaps of the hat that covered his ears.

In a spot where the ice gave way to bare rock, I ran my hands along some scars in the mountain. They were like claw marks from top to bottom. I took out my notebook and wrote a question for the park ranger.

What made those marks? I pointed to the grooves.

After reading that he wrote back, *Scrapes from glaciers.* He motioned for me to follow him, then picked up a chunk of ice from the ground. He held the ice against the side of the mountain and dragged it down the length of a groove. I shook my head, not because I thought the ranger was lying to me, but because it was so hard to picture that. It seemed like the ice would just drip off the mountain as it melted, not rake a path on its way down. The ranger nodded like he understood my disbelief.

The ice is so heavy, he wrote, *that when it slides off, it leaves these deep scratches.*

I placed my hand on the bare rock, still freezing to the touch, even though it was no longer covered with ice. Like the memory of the glaciers was so strong, the sunlight couldn't get through it.

Farther down the trail, a group had gathered on a small beach carved into the mountain, next to a waterfall. Some people held their hands out toward the waterfall, then laughed and pulled away. Grandma walked ahead of me. Before I got close to the waterfall, the spray that flew into the air chilled my face with dots of icy water. I stayed back while Grandma continued walking. The water from the fall rushed into the pool of turquoise water below. I knew without being able to hear anything that this water was noisy.

Grandma held out her hand to catch the spray of glacier water before the sea claimed it. She stood closer to the waterfall than anyone, but she didn't seem to notice the cold. When she saw me watching her, she signed, *"It's freezing!"* So she had noticed it, but hadn't backed away. I took a step toward her, then stopped. I'd leave her with this moment, face lifted before the rushing waterfall, drops of glacial water sliding down the lines on her face. I wondered if she felt like Grandpa was there next to her, feeling the cold water too.

Grandma laughed. A real laugh, one that shook her shoulders and deepened the lines around her eyes. When was the last time she'd done that? Since before Grandpa died, for sure. If it was possible that he could still be with us in some way, this is what I'd want him to see.

Even when the water is icy, the sea can melt away a drizzly November.

32

Our next stop, Skagway, was a pretty town, but it was hard to think about anything but Blue 55. Everything I'd worked for would be happening the next day. I'd gone through so much to make it happen, and then I couldn't believe it was time. At least, I hoped it would be—55 still wasn't singing. Maybe my song would work, and he'd start singing again when he heard it.

Grandma and I ate burgers and onion rings at a restaurant that used to be an old saloon. When it was time to pay, Grandma handed the waiter a fifty-dollar bill and left a big tip. *"Had some luck at the casino."*

"Nice! Keep winning, and you can live on the ship all the time."

Grandma laughed at that. *"I wish!"*

After lunch we did some sightseeing around town. A small crowd in a park watched lumberjacks with chainsaws carve upright logs into sculptures of bears and salmon. From there we wandered into the downtown area.

Grandma stopped at the door of a gift shop and asked, *"Want to look around in here?"* The shop took up most of the block and had everything from bumper stickers to T-shirts to packaged salmon. Postcards with Alaskan scenery filled a spinning rack. Right then it hit me how much I missed my family. I couldn't stand to think about how worried they were, so I'd been trying not to think about them at all. It wasn't working.

I shuffled through a few cards with animals on them, then settled on one with a picture of a breaching humpback and "Alaska" written in cursive letters in one corner.

At the cash register I paid for the postcard with change from my pocket and stepped aside. With a pen I borrowed from the counter, I filled out my home address on the three blank lines on the back of the postcard. Next to that was space for a short note.

Dear Mom, Dad, and Tristan,
    I wanted to let you know I'm thinking about you. Please don't worry about us. Sorry for leaving without telling you.

I just had to find the whale.

Love,

Iris

When the customer at the counter left with his bag, I showed the cashier the postcard and tapped the "Place stamp here" square in the corner. She pointed across the street and said, "Post office."

I found Grandma browsing through the T-shirts. *"Just going across the street to mail this,"* I told her. *"Be right back."*

She held up a green "I Brake for Moose" T-shirt to check the size. *"Okay, I'll stay here and look around."*

I hadn't been to many post offices—just the one near home sometimes when one of my parents had to mail a package—but this had to be the tiniest post office in the land. It looked more like a little cabin, with wood paneling all around the inside walls. Only one person worked at the counter, and a few people stood in line. I wanted to ask if I could go ahead of everyone since all I needed was one stamp, but that was probably against post office rules. Instead of hanging on to the card to send later, I gave it to the postal worker to mail for me right then. By the time it got to my house, our trip would be almost over. The important part, anyway. If

Blue 55 was in Appleton like he should be, I'd be meeting him soon. Nothing else would matter after that. My family would know I'd been thinking of them, and not just of myself.

I didn't see how I'd get any sleep that night, thinking about how close I was to Blue 55, about all I'd done and how far I'd come. We'd be sailing into the sanctuary's waters soon. We might even be sailing by Blue 55 right then. He needed to sing again so I'd know. I opened the sound file on my phone so I could feel his song against my hand, and wished he was out there joining in.

If I didn't get to sleep by six, I'd go out to the front of the ship to watch us pull into Appleton.

At some point I did fall asleep. When I woke up, Grandma's bed was empty.

I sat up in bed, wondering where she could be. Maybe she was just out for a walk. That was the kind of thing she would do. But in the middle of the night? I grabbed my coat and wandered into the hallway. Empty.

Maybe something came up, and she didn't want to bother me. Or could this be like the time she took off for the beach without telling anyone? But she couldn't have gone far—we literally were on the ocean. I couldn't think of where to look for her. It was too late for any classes to be going on. Usually if she wasn't in the cabin, she was out on deck reading or watching the water. It'd be too dark to see much, but I couldn't think of where else to check.

The ship was as busy in the middle of the night as it was during the day. People swam in the pools and mingled around the bars, carrying their umbrella drinks.

I had to try to think like Grandma. Where would she want to go?

The casino. Even though I wouldn't be allowed in, I'd have a good chance of spotting her from the wide doorways. A crew member kept his eye on me as I stood at the edge of the casino entrance. I guess to make sure I wasn't going to run in and try my luck at the slot machines. The place was packed, even in the middle of the night. As far as I could tell through the haze of cigarette smoke, Grandma wasn't there. Same thing on the opposite side, when I circled around to the other entrance. Some of the machines weren't visible from where I was, so I'd check back later if I had to.

It was impossible for one person to search the whole ship, but I looked everywhere I could think of. I even tried the internet café and the library. When I didn't find Grandma at the pool, out on deck, or in any of the diners, I went back to the cabin to see if she'd returned.

Still not there. She should've left me a note, at least. Nothing on the desk except the daily schedule and Jojo's business card. I turned to the back of the card, where Jojo had written *Customer relations can page me if you need anything.*

Did she mean at any time? Of course she would be asleep, but this was important. This wasn't a call for extra towels or a room cleaning. What if something had happened to Grandma?

I ran back to the elevator, clutching Jojo's card. Maybe the people at the customer service desk wouldn't need to call her, but they'd find Grandma somehow.

Surprisingly I wasn't the only one who needed customer service that time of night. Three people were in line ahead of me. They couldn't possibly have anything as important as a missing grandma. While I waited I tried to think of where else to look.

Finally it was my turn. When I stepped off the carpet onto the concrete floor in front of the counter, vibrations tickled my feet. I slipped out of my shoes and stood there in my socks. Music was playing somewhere nearby. Loud music, with those low bass sounds that really shook a radio speaker.

The man behind the counter waved to get my attention, saying something that looked like "Can I help you?" I shook my head and stepped aside to let the passenger behind me take his turn. The thread of a memory waited for me to grab on to it. Something about what Grandma had said that first night on the ship.

The carpet muffled some of the music, but there was enough of a vibration for me to follow. It grew stronger as I ran, shoes in hand, toward the stern.

In front of the Tipsy Marlin Bar, I stopped. During the day it was always empty. Not now. The bar was packed with people, dancing and laughing and holding drinks. At the front of that crowd, in the lights of the stage, hands flying, was Grandma. A banner hanging from the ceiling read "Tipsy Marlin Karaoke Night."

As far as I knew, there weren't any other Deaf people on board, but everyone was watching Grandma. This must have been going on for a long time, because she'd taught the audience some sign language. The words "Break it down" appeared on the lyrics screen, which Grandma signed. Then everyone did some weird dance and signed together, *"Stop, Hammer time!"*

It was like Grandma was signing a language everyone in the world understood. Mom wouldn't believe this. She'd been wanting Grandma to make friends, and now it looked like she'd made a whole roomful.

Watching Grandma reminded me of the humpback whales that leaped out of the ocean. The symphony players. If someone could write Grandma's signing on sheet music, every color would be splashed all the way up and down the musical scale, and off the page.

I was too amazed to be mad at her. As I stood there holding my shoes in one hand, I wondered if my own family would feel the same way about what I'd done. I'd wandered off too, much farther than Grandma ever had. But if they saw that this was where I was supposed to be, that I was doing exactly what I was supposed to be doing, maybe they'd understand just a little. The way Grandma looked then—that was how I'd feel when I met Blue 55.

She'd also taught the audience how to do Deaf applause. Instead of clapping when the song ended, everyone waved their raised hands. As Grandma stepped off the stage, she got a standing ovation.

I didn't care if I wasn't allowed in a bar. I ran to Grandma and hugged her, then stepped back. "How . . . ?" I couldn't even finish my sentence.

"I'm sorry to worry you. I didn't think I'd be gone for so long. I couldn't sleep, so I got up to take a walk around the ship, and stumbled upon karaoke night."

"I mean . . ." I pointed to the stage. "*That. How did you do that?*"

"*After I watched some of the performers, someone tried to get me to go up and sing. I told them I'm Deaf, and they asked me to sign the songs with them. Pretty soon I was doing my own performance and getting the crowd to join in. Looks like everyone had fun, right?*"

Yes, it did look like everyone had had fun. More importantly, Grandma had.

I'd wanted to make that trip by myself. For the first time I was happy that a plan of mine failed, so I could be right there with Grandma.

33

The chattering of dolphins filled the water as the pod raced past him. They'd played like this throughout the day, falling behind and darting ahead, then leaping in front of him.

He led them to a school of fish. They were too large for the whale to filter through his baleen and swallow, but they made a feast for the dolphins. While they ate, the whale circled the fish to keep them close.

The pod swam slowly, weighed down by the meal. The whale glided alongside a dolphin and lowered his head, an invitation to swim onto his back. This is how they communicated, soundlessly. The dolphin threw herself onto the whale. He sank down to keep her just below the surface, then propelled his body through the water, ahead of the pod.

This happened once in a great while, this meeting with dolphins. They would find him and spend the day leaping and racing alongside him, chattering. If only he knew what drew them to him, he would try to bring them closer more often. Was it a sound he'd made that was like theirs? If it was, he would sing that sound again and again. He wasn't like them—they didn't sing the same songs—but they understood each other in a way. He knew they had fun diving alongside him, jumping onto his back for a ride through the surf.

The whale dove down, then up to the surface, bursting out of the ocean. The water splashed high around him when he crashed down on his side. He rejoined the pod, notes of joy waving through his song.

If they could play like this every day, at least for a little while, he wouldn't be so lonely. But dolphins never stayed for long.

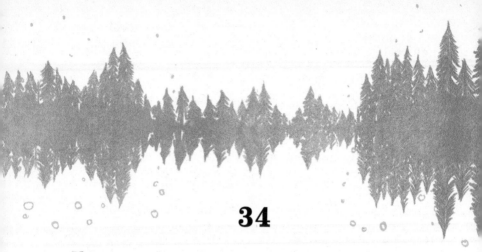

34

This was it. The day when everything I'd planned, all the work I'd done, would come together. It would be worth it because of what would happen in just a couple of hours.

Bennie joined Grandma and me for breakfast. After loading up my plate at the buffet, all I could do was stare out the window, too excited to eat.

It didn't feel like the boat was moving anymore. We were there.

"*Ready?*" Grandma signed.

I nodded but stayed in my seat, clutching my backpack. The whole reason for the trip was right ahead of me. Of course I'd have to leave the ship to get any closer to the sanctuary, but I couldn't make myself stand up. Until then I hadn't failed. Soon, that could change. Even if I did get to see the expedition, it might not work out. Maybe Blue 55 would swim away, like he had before, or avoid the boat altogether. He had no way of knowing what this meant to me. He might come and go without a glance, or not show up at all.

So many ways to fail, all right in front of me. But I had to try.

First I'd check to see how close 55 was to the sanctuary. I'd been avoiding the tracker app, since there was nothing I could do about where Blue 55 was. But now, it was worth finding out if we had to hurry off the ship right then or take our time. That was if he was singing at all.

Instead of the dotted line that had been on the screen the last time I'd looked, a solid black line traced 55's path. When I saw the blinking blue dot that showed where he was, I closed the tracker app and set my phone facedown on the table. That solid line I'd been so desperate to see had finally appeared. I just didn't expect it to be so far away.

I picked up the phone again, even though I didn't want to look. If I left it on the table, it didn't have to be true yet. Maybe the program just needed to refresh. But no, when I reopened it, there was the current time and date. Blue 55 was singing again, but from far away. One of the detours he sometimes took, for reasons no one knew. I tried to push away the thought that crept into my mind: I wasn't going to meet Blue 55.

Grandma and Bennie looked at me with questions on their faces, waiting for me to explain what was wrong. All I could do was hold the phone out for them to see.

"*Washington?*" Grandma signed.

The sanctuary had to know the news. What were they going to do? I opened up their website and found a new post: "Operation Tag 55—Headed South!"

Well, folks, nature is unpredictable! We're relieved to find out that Blue 55 is alive and singing, but the bad news is he's nowhere near Appleton as usual. For some reason he changed course, and is swimming off the Washington coast, heading toward Oregon. We will still go forward with the tagging, but it won't happen here. A couple of us will be flying to the marine mammal sanctuary in Lighthouse Bay, Oregon, where we expect Blue 55 will be in a few days. We'll work with the staff there to go out to tag 55 with a tracker.

No mention of the song that I'd made for him. When I opened my email to send Andi a message to ask about it, I found that she'd already written to me.

Dear Iris,

Well, we have good news and bad news, which you know if you're keeping up with Blue 55. Here's a link to our latest post in case you haven't seen it, and to Lighthouse Bay's sanctuary. It's a great place, one that I think would be good for 55 to hang out in for a while if he wants to, but we'll see what he does. Since they're in warmer waters, they take care of whales and dolphins year-round. It'll be interesting to see if Blue 55 interacts at all with the animals there. He'd have a captive audience, you could say.

I did pass along your song to them, and I'm sorry to say they don't want to play it. We'll have the hydrophone and speaker aboard the boat so we can listen for the whale, but the team wants to just get out there, tag him, and get back to the sanctuary without adding anything else to the plan. They're worried that playing the song over the boat's speaker would make it harder to hear Blue 55. I mentioned playing your song afterward, but they didn't think it was important, since the goal is to tag him with the tracker. I disagree with them and think it'd be interesting to find out if he responded to the recording. But since we'll be at their sanctuary now, it's really their call.

Sorry I don't have better news for you. We'll still broadcast the expedition online, so you'll be able to watch when and if we meet Blue 55. And whenever he does come to Appleton again, we'll play your song for him.

Andi

I wanted to throw my phone at the wall and watch Andi's dumb message shatter into a thousand pieces. Instead I pounded the table and shoved my chair back. I couldn't stand to think about what this meant. I handed my phone to Bennie so she and Grandma could read the update.

Before he changed course Blue 55 had finally been swimming toward a friend. I'd felt like we were in this together, both heading toward the place where we'd find each other. But it was just me, all along.

Bennie showed me the screen of her own phone, where she'd typed *Now what?*

I shrugged. There was nothing to do. This didn't make sense! Nothing in the world was singing back to this whale, except for one Deaf girl.

I'd check out the sanctuary Andi mentioned, at least

to see where Blue 55 would be. Maybe I'd watch the tagging expedition online after all. Which I could have done if I'd stayed home, with my family and Wendell and a bowl of popcorn.

After Grandma handed my phone back to me, I clicked on the Lighthouse Bay link from the message. The screen filled with a picture of a blue bay next to a tall white lighthouse topped with a red roof. A page labeled "The Residents" showed a picture of each animal at the sanctuary, along with a brief description. Some of them were free to come and go, as long as they were healthy. Part of the sanctuary was like a hospital for injured and sick animals, and they lived in either indoor pools or in sea pens until they were rehabilitated and ready to return to the open ocean. The bay was made from an underwater canyon, almost as big as the Grand Canyon. So even the water near the docks and the shore was miles deep, instead of sloping from shallow to deep water like at the beaches I was used to.

Some of the animals were retired performers from places like SeaWorld. They were too old or sick to continue doing shows, but they didn't know how to hunt for food in the wild. They lived in the large sea pens so they had plenty of room to swim around but still had people to toss fish to them. Without being asked, two of the dolphins there still performed their old show routine three times a day, right on schedule. A beluga whale whose tail had been injured by a propeller lived in another outdoor pen. There were also albino animals, such as a pink dolphin and a seal. Their color made them too obvious to hunt or avoid predators, and they'd been abandoned by their families.

It reminded me of the TV movie about Rudolph the Red-Nosed Reindeer that played every year at Christmastime. Here was the Island of Misfit Toys for ocean mammals.

Blue 55 wasn't injured or sick like any of those animals, but maybe he'd feel at home and stick around for a while if he heard a familiar song. I didn't understand what was so hard about playing the song after the tagging.

The news page on the site had an announcement— "The Return of Mara"—about a young whale they'd helped rescue two years earlier. She was found stranded on a nearby beach, and staff from the Lighthouse Bay sanctuary was able to return her to the ocean. They weren't sure she'd survive long after that, though— she was barely old enough to make it without her mother, who wasn't anywhere around. They named her Mara and tagged her so they could track how she was doing. She surprised everyone by making it on her own. Each summer since then, the sanctuary staff celebrated when Mara returned to Lighthouse Bay, where the people who'd rescued her could watch her swim. She was there at the bay right then, and was a blue whale, like 55's mother.

I wondered if Blue 55 and Mara would be able to communicate a little, if they spent enough time together. She hadn't interacted with other whales much. No telling how much language she had or didn't have. Maybe they could be like Bennie and me and become friends, even though they spoke different languages.

Yes, Lighthouse Bay would be the perfect place for Blue 55. And here I was, more than a thousand miles away. I couldn't believe it. If only I'd known earlier that this might happen, I could have flown to whatever airport was closest to the Oregon sanctuary and made my way from there. Instead I'd walked right onto the ship that was going to keep me from meeting Blue 55.

My plan was crumbling like the wire insulation in that radio I'd worked on at home. All the parts were in place, but with nothing to connect them. I traced the etched whale on the compass with my finger as I thought about what to do. No point in leaving the ship any longer. My whole reason for being there was swimming away.

"We'll think of something," Grandma told me. Bennie nodded in agreement.

I wanted to believe them, even though it was hopeless. All the new problems were wrapped up in my head in a tangled ball I couldn't unravel. If only Blue 55 had been singing lately, we'd have known where he was and in what direction he was headed, instead of getting hit with the news on the day I was supposed to meet him. Maybe it was a last-minute decision and he didn't feel like telling anyone, like Grandma when she took off for the beach that day.

Bennie tapped me and signed, *"Paper. I forgot mine."* I handed her my notepad. She set it in the middle of the table between her and Grandma.

"Phone, too," Grandma signed. *"Show me that sanctuary."*

Grandma scrolled through the Lighthouse Bay site, then opened a map on the phone and scribbled some dates on the notepad.

"If we rent a car and drive to the sanctuary after getting off the ship in San Francisco, we'll miss him." Grandma

scrolled up the map. *"Let's see how far it is from Cape Oliver."*

Before ending the cruise in San Francisco, the ship would stop at one port in Oregon. Bennie brought up a map on her own phone and found the distance to the sanctuary from that last stop, Cape Oliver.

Grandma jotted down more dates and a schedule. *"We'll have a chance if we drive there from Cape Oliver. Maybe we'll even be early. If that's the case, we'll stick around until he gets there."*

"What if we can't get back here on time?" Even if the ship stayed in port all day, we probably wouldn't make it back after driving all that way, meeting Blue 55, then driving back to the ship. I didn't know how we'd get all our things from the cabin and get back to San Francisco to fly home if we really did miss the boat. Plus, Grandma was enjoying the cruise. I didn't want her to miss out on the rest of it because of me.

Grandma shrugged. *"We'll figure it out. Meeting the whale is the important thing, right?"*

Maybe I wouldn't even get to meet the whale after all, but there wasn't a better plan. Then I thought of a way I could get to Lighthouse Bay on my own. There was no reason for Grandma to miss any of the cruise.

I spelled out *"b-u-s"* and pointed to Cape Oliver on the map. Then I wrote: *I could go by myself, and Grandma can stay here.*

Grandma leaned over to read my note. *"That's too far. I don't want you going all that way yourself."*

I tapped the thumb of a five handshape on my chest to argue back, *"I'll be fine."*

Before Grandma could answer back, Bennie touched my arm and signed, *"Kid,"* and pointed at me. I shrugged, wondering what she was getting at.

The ship won't leave a kid behind alone, she wrote on the notepad. *They'd have to wait for you. You can't leave the ship without your grandma anyway.*

So that wouldn't work. I really wanted Grandma to stay on board. She was happy here. She'd found fun things to do. And she was really trying to come up with a way to meet Blue 55. Maybe meeting him would make her happy too. *Okay,* I wrote, *we'll drive. But we might not make it back before the ship leaves.*

Bennie read my note, then flipped to a new page.

She smiled and wrote something down, then set the notepad on the table for us to see.

The train is faster.

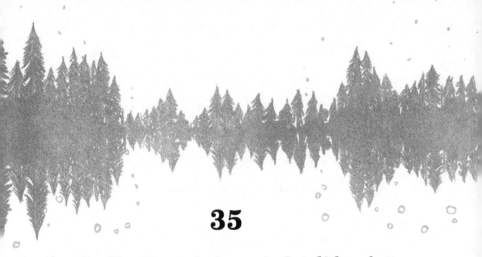

35

Now that Blue 55 was singing again, I could keep better track of where he was. But there was nothing to do except let the ship bring us closer. Even if we did get to the sanctuary on time, I wouldn't get to see him. The expedition crew wasn't even willing to take a speaker on board to play the song, so they sure weren't going to pick up a stray girl. Maybe I'd at least get to see Blue 55 swimming, if he decided to hang around the sanctuary. Even from a distance, I could recognize his blow spout.

That would have to be enough, since he wasn't going to hear the song I'd made for him. He still wouldn't know anyone heard him. When I got back home, I'd send the song to more sanctuaries along his path. Maybe one of them would play it when he swam by. I wouldn't be there to meet him, but he'd know he wasn't alone.

The train that Bennie showed us was a scenic ride that a lot of cruise passengers took during the port stop at Cape Oliver. The round-trip ride took three hours, and it stopped at the halfway point for a break, so people could get out to take pictures and buy lunch. Instead of getting on the train to ride back to the ship, Grandma and I would catch a shuttle to Lighthouse Bay. If we got there before Blue 55 did, we'd hang around until he arrived, even if it meant missing the rest of the cruise.

I didn't want to think about the other thing that might happen: we could get to Lighthouse Bay to find that Blue 55 had already come and gone.

That afternoon I joined Bennie and Sura on the bridge for the fjord tour. Sura would make announcements about the scenery and wildlife around us as the ship sailed through a narrow passage with walls of glaciers on either side.

Bennie said a local pilot would get on board to help the captain. I'd thought pilots were only for flying planes, but it turned out that was also what they call people who steer ships. Anyway, this local pilot who knew the area a lot better than the captain would guide the ship around the ice so we wouldn't crash into anything.

The ship eased into the narrow passage of the fjord. Ice bobbed in the water, pushed aside by the waves created by the ship. Seals lounged at the base of the mountain and on ice floes. The ice reflected more shades of blue I didn't have names for. I never knew snow-cone-syrup blue was a color found in nature. I closed my eyes for a few seconds to see if I could still picture it. Maybe I'd never see another glacier again, so I wanted to hold on to that color.

Bennie tapped my arm, then pointed to the right after I opened my eyes. *"Watch,"* she signed. At first I didn't see what I was supposed to be looking at. Then blocks of ice tumbled into the water next to us, making waves that splashed onto the rocks.

I pointed and shrugged to ask Bennie how she knew that was going to happen. She pointed to her ear. So they'd heard it? Some kind of sound warned of the glacier breaking apart. More chunks of ice crashed into the water. Melting ice always looked so quiet, but this was noisy. The counter in front of us wasn't vibrating when I touched it, so it was a different kind of sound than the foghorn. Bennie pointed to a glacier next to us, then wrote *calving* on our notepad. I looked back at the glacier, still wondering what such a crashing and falling apart sounded like. She signed something that looked like *"break"* and then *"watch."*

A giant block of ice separated from the glacier and floated away from the mountain.

On the page where Bennie had written *calving*, I added *Like a baby glacier.*

Yep, a glacier calf! she wrote.

What does it sound like?

She covered her ears and said, "Loud."

What kind of loud? I wrote.

Really loud.

But there were all kinds of loud; I knew that much. Was it a scream? A crash? Maybe the opposite of a crash, whatever that was, since this was a ripping apart.

Bennie tapped the pen against her mouth like she was thinking. She could tell I wanted to know more, even without my asking her. Then she wrote, *Thunder.*

I never would have guessed that two totally different events could make the same sound.

She wrote more notes and used some signs to tell me what her mom was announcing. *Air bubbles have been trapped under the ice for hundreds of years. All that pressure squishes them out of shape. When the ice melts or breaks away, the bubbles make a loud pop.*

Like they were screaming out after being trapped for so long.

I pointed to the seals and wrote, *The noise doesn't bother them?*

She shook her head. *They hang out here on purpose. The glacier noise makes it hard for orcas to hear them.*

Like with the humpbacks' bubble net feeding, I wondered how the seals figured out that a noise could help them. Instead of using it to get food like the whales did, the seals used it to avoid *becoming* food.

The ship inched along through the fjord. Looking ahead, I didn't see how we'd be able to squeeze through the narrow space between the mountains. As we got closer I saw that there was plenty of water on either side of us. Still, the pilot had to drive slowly because of all the floating ice. Most looked like chunks that the ship could easily knock aside, but Bennie said we were just looking at the tops of those chunks and that most of the ice was below the surface.

We were only partway through the fjord when the ship stopped completely. The pilot talked to the captain while pointing at the water ahead of us, then shook her head. Then the captain picked up the microphone.

The engine jerked, and we started inching backward. The front of the ship turned bit by bit to the left.

I shrugged at Bennie, then pantomimed turning a big wheel, even though no one actually turned a wheel to steer the ship. *"We're turning around?"*

Bennie pointed to the floating ice in the water and signed, *"Dangerous."* Then she took the notepad and wrote what the captain had just announced. *Sometimes you have to know when it's time to give up and turn back.*

"Did you see the glacier calving?" I asked Grandma when I got back to the room.

"No, that must have been on the other side of the ship. I saw ice rolling off the side of the mountain, but nothing breaking apart like that. What was it like?"

"Beautiful and sad at the same time." That wasn't enough. How could I possibly describe what it was like to witness a glacier tearing apart?

I sat across from Grandma and said, *"Handshape poem?"*

She didn't hesitate or dismiss it as Grandpa's thing this time. *"What shape?"* she asked.

I held up my hands into fives, like in Grandpa's tree poem, but bent my fingers into claws. A good shape for frozen things and mountains and floating ice: spread-out fingers to show something big, and bent to show the jagged peaks. It was also the handshape for signing "frozen" and "rough," so it was perfect for a poem about the icy mountain of the breaking glacier.

First I signed *"frozen,"* then reached up to trace rising and falling curves of mountaintops. My hands showed Grandma the layers of ice that pressed down and trapped the pockets of air inside. With spinning hands I showed chunks of ice tumbling down and crashing into the ocean, making rough waves. Then I held them out for the bigger block of the glacier, breaking and drifting away.

"The glacier screams, watching a piece of itself float farther and farther from home."

Grandma joined in when she could see the glacier calving too. *"The new iceberg rides the rough waves in the sea."* Her hands outlined its shape, smaller and jagged with new breaks.

I showed her that what was left of the glacier clung to the mountainside. It looked rougher then, with sharp edges marking the missing ice.

She raked her hands, as if they were claws, on the glacier and then straightened her fingers a little to draw softer waves—the scars on the ice melting. The new iceberg drifted so far away it was a speck in the ocean. *"Time and distance smooth out the memory of what was lost."*

I didn't know anymore if we were still talking about the iceberg, or about 55 and me, or my family, or Grandma and Grandpa. Maybe it was all those things.

36

I woke up early and couldn't get back to sleep, so I went to the internet café to check on Blue 55's progress. My phone couldn't connect to the Wi-Fi from our cabin.

It was so early the gelato wasn't even out yet. I'd have to work without it. The sanctuary's website didn't have any updates, so I switched over to the map that showed where 55 was. He was making progress. Too much progress. A TV screen above me showed the cruise ship's route. With the stops we'd be making along the way, 55 was going to get to Oregon long before we did if he kept up his pace.

All along I was in such a hurry to meet him, and now I just wanted him to wait for me. *Please slow down.* I touched the blinking blue dot on the screen, as if I could hold him in place. I imagined myself chasing him across the ocean forever, never getting close enough to even catch sight of his breath.

I'd tried so hard to do everything right, to do what was best for Blue 55. He needed to hear that song; I was sure of that. It looked more and more like I'd have to go back home without having played it for him or seeing him at all. The more I tried to reach him, the farther he swam away.

Before leaving I checked my email, even though I cringed while opening it. If anyone at home was in a panic about us, I wanted to send a reply that would calm them down.

The first was from Tristan.

Iris,

I still can't believe y'all did this. I know you've both told Mom you're okay, but tell me for real. Is everything all right? I don't know what I can do from here if it isn't, but tell me where you are, and we'll help you if you need it.

Write back to Dad, too. Mom says he hasn't been sleeping since you left.

Love you even though you're totally ridiculous,

Tristan

I couldn't believe Dad was so worried that he wasn't sleeping. I opened his last email to me.

Iris,

You know that record I showed you, with the whale songs? I don't know if I told you that a copy of it is in space. The Voyager space capsule. It's true. It's carrying a lot of things from Earth, including the whale song record. If there's alien life out there somewhere, the items in the capsule will let them know what life is like on Earth. Maybe one day someone will figure out what the songs mean.

I know I told you I wanted to find those whales when I heard them. But even if I had, even if they were right in front of me, I wouldn't have known what to say.

Please let me know how you're doing. Better yet, tell me where you are. I'm worried sick. You can't imagine how much I miss you.

Love,

Dad

At the breakfast buffet I found a small table near a window. I never thought I'd miss the school cafeteria, but I wondered how everyone at school was doing and what they'd been talking about at lunch while I was gone. Most of the time I felt invisible, but they had to notice I was gone, right? Maybe Nina found someone new to bother by now. I laughed and took a bite of my cheese omelet. And what about Mr. Charles? A pang of guilt hit my stomach when I realized I hadn't even thought of him much. He'd told me before that whenever I was absent, he went to work at one of the schools with more Deaf kids, helping out in classrooms or filling in for interpreters who were absent.

People around me in the buffet area stopped eating and looked up like they were all listening to something. Some of them shoveled in a last bite of food as they stood up and ran out. I finished my mango juice and followed the stampede out to the deck.

On my notepad I wrote *What's going on?* and showed it to an old woman next to me.

After reading the question she cupped her hands around her mouth and yelled, "WHALES!" at my face.

There wasn't a whale sighting announcement on the schedule for the day, but obviously whales didn't always follow a schedule. Maybe Sura had spotted them and went to the bridge to announce the unplanned whale sighting.

Each time I saw a group of passengers pointing at something, they were always on the opposite side of the ship. Sometimes they laughed and clapped. The whales must have breached, putting on a show for whoever was watching. Then I'd switch sides to get a better view of the action, and the people on the side I'd just left would do the pointing-laughing-and-clapping thing. Whales were swimming right near the ship, and I missed out on every one of them. I stamped my foot on the deck, angry all over again about the sanctuary not using my idea. Blue 55 was going to be right there, and they weren't going to play the song I'd worked so hard to make for him.

After about an hour the crowd thinned out when there were no more leaping whales to see. Passengers returned to the pools and bars and dining rooms.

The breeze chilled my face as I leaned against the railing and watched the waves. I tucked my scarf under the front of my coat. My heart beating against my hand reminded me of Blue 55's song, so I kept it there.

Yes, things had turned out terribly, but I was on a ship sailing over the ocean. Not a bad place to remarkably fail. I'd made it that far, and I'd tried really hard to help out one whale. I stared out at the water that was so calm it had to be as quiet for everyone else as it was for me.

Then a plume of teardrop-shape spray erupted. And another spray, smaller than the first.

The shadows of two whale backs brushed the surface. Humpbacks, if I remembered right from what Sura and Bennie had taught me. One large and one small. A mother and a calf. I looked around at the other passengers. No one else seemed to have noticed. It was almost like it hadn't happened. Maybe I'd imagined the whole thing.

When I looked back, the Y shape of two whale flukes lifted up from the surface, then sank down.

"Thank you," I signed to them. Then I laughed. Those whales showed up right when I needed to see them. I wasn't mad anymore about missing the breaching humpbacks with the rest of the crowd.

The mother and calf sighting was mine alone.

"Gelato time?" Bennie asked when I caught up with her later. It did sound good, since I hadn't eaten for about two hours.

The ship was on its way to the next stop, Icy Harbor. We planned to stay aboard, since Bennie said there wasn't much to see there.

"What flavor?" I asked when we got to the café.

"Church," she signed.

I held back a giggle and wrote, *Not for me. Tastes like bricks.*

Bennie's forehead crinkled with confusion, then

she pointed to the "Chocolate" label behind the glass. I showed her how to draw circles with the letter *C* on the back of her hand, instead of tapping it for "church." She laughed at her mistake when she caught on. I wished Mr. Charles had been there to see it.

After we stopped giggling we picked up a chocolate and a pistachio and spooned some of each into the other's bowl until we each had a perfect chocolate-pistachio blend.

We settled into our seats by the window and checked out the map of 55's path. The blue dot seemed to be racing to Oregon. How could he have covered so many miles since I'd last checked?

Bennie looked worried too and checked the ship's route on the TV screen like I had. *"Maybe he'll slow down."*

"Yeah, hopefully," I answered. *"Nothing I can do from here."* I sighed and brought up my email to see what was new from home.

After asking me to reply back with more than "We're fine," Mom wrote:

I went to the school to collect your work for you to catch up on when you're back. I don't like you missing so much. I had to think of something to tell the office that didn't sound completely ridiculous, like that you and your grandmother took off on a trip to who knows where. I told them there'd been a family emergency, and you'd be back next week. That's all I knew from what you and Grandma have told me. Oh, and when I was in the office, I saw that girl Nina. Isn't that who you got in trouble for shoving? She seemed really nice. She says she hopes you're okay and that you inspired her to learn sign language.

Usually when people use a phrase like "fell over laughing," they mean it as a figure of speech. "I laughed really hard" is what they mean. But I actually fell over laughing at that. I sat on the floor next to the computer table and wiped tears from my eyes. Whenever I tried to explain to Bennie what was so funny, I'd start laughing all over again.

Finally I stood up and turned the computer screen to Bennie so she could read the email, then I pointed to the last line. *"She's terrible,"* I signed. On the computer's notepad, I added, *She's always signing and signing, but I never have any idea what she means. It's like she gets*

*worse every day instead of better. Maybe that library book
she checked out is for some other country's sign language,
because it's nothing I know.*

Bennie shrugged, then typed, *It's nice that she wants
to learn anyway.*

*Not that nice if she won't even listen when I tell her I don't
understand her. Anyway, not much point if it's that bad.*

After reading my message Bennie wrote, *Probably
no worse than you speaking whale, right?*

37

Bennie suggested we go swimming the day the ship was docking in Icy Harbor. The pools wouldn't be as crowded as they usually were, since a lot of people would be leaving the ship for a few hours. Luckily Grandma had told me to pack a swimsuit before we left home. It hadn't occurred to me I'd need one on a ship that would be sailing past glaciers, but the pools on board were heated. Grandma didn't want to swim, but she would sit out on deck and read, right after her Zumba class.

Bennie was right—the pool wasn't crowded at all. A few people sat around in the hot tub, and one man sat on a floating chair in the pool, a beer can in the chair's cup holder.

I jumped in and swam the length of the pool, then floated on my back. It had been so long since I'd been swimming. When we lived at the coast, we used to go out all the time. Tristan and I would bodysurf the waves or float in our inner tubes if the water was calm enough. The current would carry us so far down the beach our house was just a yellow speck in the distance. Tristan always kept change in the zippered pocket of his swim trunks so we could each buy a cone at the ice cream stand to eat while hiking back home.

A splash of water snapped my mind back to the cruise ship's pool. Bennie laughed and backed away. I tried to pretend I was mad, but a laugh escaped as I splashed her back. She ducked under the surface before the water could hit her, so I waited until she came up for air, then got her good. Before she could get me back, I took a deep breath and swam to the other side of the pool. I popped out of the water and held up my hand to signal Bennie to stop.

"Do you feel that?" I asked.

She shrugged. *"What?"* She backed up a little, as if she suspected my answer might be a splash to her face.

I placed my hand flat on the surface. Something other than our splashing or the ship's engines was moving the water, with the steady rhythm of music. It was still just us and the man on the float in the pool. Nothing I could see that could've been vibrating the water like a radio.

"*Music*," I signed. We'd talked so much about the whale song, that was a sign she'd picked up.

"Oh, that." She pointed to something on the other side of the floating chair. I swam to see what she was talking about. A blue-and-white cylinder floated in the water next to the man.

Bennie swam up next to me and pointed at the object again, then signed, "*Music*."

A speaker. There weren't any wires connected to it, so it must have been Bluetooth. My parents had one stuck to their shower wall with suction cups.

The man's phone rested in a cup holder. The music that played from there was coming through the speaker.

I signed "*buy*" and "*here*" to Bennie, to ask if the gift shop on board sold the speakers. She shook her head.

The ship was still moving, sailing past mountains in the distance. But soon we'd stop in Icy Harbor. Bennie waved to get my attention, but I held up a hand to ask her to wait. I didn't want to let go of the plan that was forming in my head. I imagined throwing a speaker into the water to play 55's song for him. Maybe I could really do it. The song was with me all the time. Not just the memory of it, from when I'd held my hand on the speaker while it played. The sound file was on my phone. I could play it for him, if I just had a way to carry the sound to where he was swimming.

If I'd had any idea I might need a speaker, I'd have brought one from home. I could throw the Bluetooth into the water after connecting the signal to my phone. Or I would've salvaged parts from the radio in that Admiral set in my closet to make a speaker. Then I'd have to make it waterproof somehow. . . .

Bennie followed me when I climbed out of the pool to dry off and get my phone from my bag. I typed out a message and showed her my phone. *I want to get off in Icy Harbor after all. I need to get a few things.* As soon as she read the message, I started making a list.

She shook two O handshapes to remind me there was nothing there. No stores or good restaurants.

I looked out at the town we were approaching. *All I need is a junkyard.*

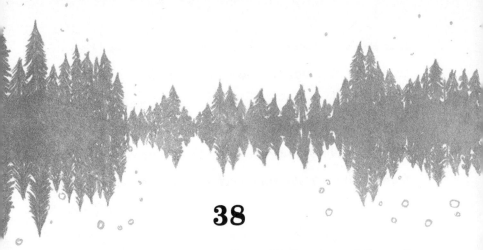

38

Sura wanted to stay on board but told the crew at the exit that Bennie could go with Grandma and me into Icy Harbor.

Bennie hadn't been to the junkyard before, but she knew it wasn't close to where the cruise ship stopped. Not much of a tourist attraction. It wasn't really a junkyard, but more of a dump, which was even better since I wouldn't have to pay for anything. But it could be messy since people dropped off trash there.

A couple of shuttles were parked near the harbor, ready to take passengers to whatever there was to see in town.

Bennie and I took a seat up front after boarding a shuttle, and Grandma asked the driver, "The dump, please," as if it were a totally normal request from a tourist.

I don't know what he said to her, but she handed

him some money from her purse, and it looked like she said, "It's important." She took a seat then, across from Bennie and me.

Bennie was right—there wasn't much in that town. A few people got out when the shuttle driver stopped at a bar, and more got out at an area that had some shops and a fishing pier. About ten minutes later, the driver pulled up to the Icy Harbor Dump.

Grandma signed at the same time she talked to the driver. *We won't be long. Will you wait for us?* He checked his watch and held up ten fingers, then waved a hand around like he was tracing a road. He had his route to get back to.

Whether or not this place had what I needed, ten minutes was enough time to figure it out.

The dump looked sort of like Moe's Junk Emporium, but with more things in piles. Maybe that was stuff no one wanted. Instead of a trailer for an office, there was an old school bus that was more rust-colored than yellow. Next to the bus stood a rickety wooden shed with the word PAINT in red letters over the entrance, and a dead appliance section like at Moe's.

A man with a bright red face and small eyes stepped off the bus-office. He looked like a lobster who had transformed into a human. Also, he looked like he probably ate at restaurants like the Cattle Prod. He and Moe would be good friends. As I ran up to him, he started to say something, and I pointed to my ear and showed him a list I'd written out. His blue work shirt had "Giblet" embroidered on the pocket. Grandma and Bennie came up after me. Giblet touched the first item on the list—a radio—then pointed to a plywood structure with an "Electronics" sign. I asked Grandma to look around for some kind of plastic container to hold the speaker parts. A small cooler would work, if I could seal the lid closed somehow. Something smaller that I could carry in my backpack would be easier. A PVC pipe would work, as long as it had the cap pieces to seal off the ends. I'd have to drill a hole in it somehow for the wires to poke through. Bennie ran with me to the electronics shed. Before going in I pushed on the side a little to make sure it wasn't going to topple over with us in it.

Looking over all the scattered electronics made me miss my room again. It didn't matter that I'd never let my collection get so disorganized or that most of it wasn't in my room anymore. Right then I missed it all. I missed home. I wanted to see my parents and Tristan. I wanted to visit the antique shop and see if my Philco was still there. I wanted to see Mr. Gunnar. It hadn't been that long since I'd been inside the store, but so much had happened since then, it was hard to imagine everything at home staying the same while so much had happened with me.

Bennie waved to snap me back to our time-limited shopping trip. The radios and stereos at the dump weren't nearly as old as what I usually repaired, but that was good. Tearing into a boom box from the 1980s wouldn't bother me like pulling a speaker out of an antique radio would. I turned a boom box around and twisted a finger to show Bennie I wanted to take out the screws. She gave me a thumbs-up and ran back to Giblet.

While I waited for Bennie, I looked around the piles of stuff for something smaller. The boom box speaker could work, but it was bigger than I wanted. Whatever I ended up making, I'd have to carry it with me to Lighthouse Bay, if we did get there on time. In the corner of the shed, I found the perfect thing—a handheld cassette player. People played music on them before CDs, and long before we could download music on computers and phones.

Bennie came back with Grandma and gave me the screwdriver. Grandma handed me a plastic thermos. It wasn't the kind you'd pour the drink out of into a mug, but the kind that was like a tall cup with a lid. A hinged spout lifted up for drinking. I'd check later to make sure no water would get in. It could be exactly what I needed. After removing the speaker from the cassette player, I slid it into the thermos. It fit, by a hair. The wires would thread through the drinking hole. I thanked Grandma and Bennie, then stuck the thermos in my backpack and signed, *"Headphones."* They glanced around the shed with me, until Bennie picked up a tangle of headphones that was like a pile of thin snakes. I held my backpack open for her to throw in the whole bundle. I'd only need one set, but there wasn't time for untangling. And it was always good to have a spare.

From there I ran toward a pile of pipes and overturned toilets. Next to a rusty pipe were a few tubes of leftover caulk. The ones without caps wouldn't be any good. The caulk inside would have dried up. I picked up the two that were still capped. Each one felt like it had more than I'd need. One was the white caulk that people used for the edges of sinks and bathtubs, and the other was the clear silicone kind. I uncapped the clear tube and squeezed out a bit to check that it hadn't dried out, then recapped it and threw it into my backpack.

Bennie turned toward the shuttle, then looked back at me and pantomimed honking a horn. Grandma waved to the driver and held up a finger, asking him to wait another minute for us. Happy as I was to find the dump, I didn't want to get abandoned there.

Giblet walked over to see how we were doing, and I pointed to the last item on my list. The wire I could salvage from the electronics there wouldn't be enough. I needed long strands of wire.

He waved for me to follow him. I told Grandma and Bennie to go ahead to the shuttle and that I'd meet them back there in a minute. Giblet led me to a section of big wooden spools. He tapped a wire-wrapped spool, then held a hand up to his ear as if it were a telephone. I knelt down and held the end of the wire, which was coated with black plastic for insulation. Perfect. The spool looked like it'd held hundreds of feet of wire when it was full. Not much was left, but it still had a lot more than I needed. I signed *"Thank you"* while mouthing the words to Giblet, then unrolled the wire from the spool. With the bundle of black wire wrapped around my hand, I ran and leaped onto the shuttle for the ride back to the cruise ship.

I had my waterproof speaker. Now I just had to put it together.

39

Bennie sat with me in our cabin to help with the speaker. Once we'd gotten back I realized I wouldn't be able to work without a screwdriver and something to strip the ends of the wire. Bennie came back with a small set of screwdrivers borrowed from the ship's electrician and some wire cutters—even better than the scissors I'd asked for. I assembled the speaker pretty quickly, then attached some of the long wires. While I worked, Bennie untangled a set of headphones. All I needed from them was a connector that would plug into my phone jack. After trimming down the headphone wires, I stripped off a little of the plastic coating, then twisted the ends together with the telephone wire. I plugged the speaker into my phone and brought up the sound file that held Blue 55's song. Bennie smiled at the song that played, made of musical instruments, the calls of ocean animals, and a bit of our own humming voices tuned to fifty-five hertz.

The bathroom sink was small, but it had enough room to test the thermos. I filled the sink with water and pushed the thermos down into it. The lid was good—when I removed it, the inside of the thermos was dry. The only part I'd have to seal would be the drinking hole, around the wires I'd pull through it.

Bennie held the thermos as I placed the assembled speaker inside and threaded the long wires through the spout. After twisting on the lid, I squeezed the clear caulk in the space around the wires. It didn't feel like it was heavy enough to sink underwater, just bob under the surface a bit. But just in case, the caulk would keep water from getting in.

The caulk wouldn't be totally dry until the next day, so I had to make sure the spout stayed out of the water until then. Now to test it in deeper water. *"Back to the pool."*

After changing back into our swimsuits and returning to the pool, Bennie got in while I sat on the edge with my phone. While the song played I checked the speaker to make sure it was working. The thermos in my hand hummed with Blue 55's song.

I placed the speaker into the pool and asked Bennie, *"Can you hear it?"*

She nodded. Other people who were swimming must have heard it too. Heads turned in our direction as the music played.

I pointed down, wondering if Bennie would hear it underwater. She ducked below the surface, then came back up a few seconds later and twisted a hand from side to side, like she was saying "Sort of." Maybe it wouldn't matter, since whales could hear better than we could, but I'd feel better knowing the song was traveling through water. Bennie pointed to the phone, then raised a thumbs-up a few times. As I pushed the volume's up button on the side of the phone, the song vibrated stronger and stronger in my hand. More people turned to look at us.

Bennie smiled and waved me into the pool. She took a deep breath and went underwater again, and I followed. The vibrations of the song for Blue 55 trembled in the water. The waves of the song rose and faded, following the pattern I'd made that I hoped was close to his.

I let the song continue to play as I swam beneath it, then floated on my back in the water. Here was a song that 55 might recognize. As long as we reached the bay on time, he would hear it in a few days.

Before the ship pulled away from Icy Harbor that

evening, I connected my phone to the Wi-Fi. Not to check Blue 55's tracker—I did wonder, but at the same time didn't want to know. Wherever he was swimming then, there wasn't anything I could do about it. Grandma and I would get to Lighthouse Bay, and *somehow* I'd play the song for him.

But I'd been thinking about adding more of myself to the song. I wished I could share my own language with him, but that wasn't possible. It would have to be enough that he could hear a little of my voice on the song I'd made, through the speaker I'd built.

I never liked talking out loud in front of people, but for some reason I didn't mind doing it for Blue 55. I downloaded a voice modulator like the app on Bennie's phone, then clicked record and spoke into the phone: "Hi, it's Iris. I'm here."

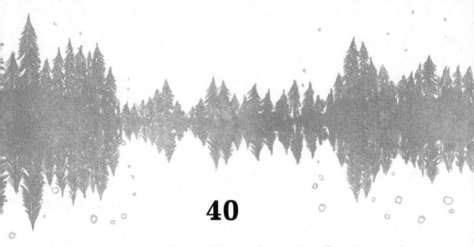

40

Since it might be our last night on the cruise, Grandma and I took our time standing out on deck before going to bed. We probably wouldn't be able to fall asleep for a while anyway, thinking about our side trip to Lighthouse Bay.

I'd never seen a night so dark. Wendell would have loved it. So many more stars than we could see at home. It looked like one of the glaciers had shattered onto the sky, dotting the blackness with shards of ice. I scanned for the unblinking brightness of Jupiter. It was harder to find in the star-crowded sky, and of course it wouldn't be in the same place as when Wendell showed me. Or maybe it was that I was in a different place. Too much had changed since then. Sometimes it felt like I'd just left home, but I'd been away long enough for planets to shift in the sky. At the same time things hadn't changed much at all. I was still so far away from the whale I'd set out to find.

If I'd been at home right then, I could have been on the Jacksons' balcony with Wendell, looking at Jupiter with him.

Then I spotted it, way off to the left, as clearly as if Wendell had been sitting there pointing it out to me. He was probably in bed asleep, but I liked the thought that maybe he was looking at Jupiter right then too.

I hadn't planned to get online again, but I decided to send one more email.

Dear Wendell,

Thinking of you because my odds of succeeding are astronomical. Ha-ha, get it?

About that planet you want to find—it was kicked out of the solar system millions of years ago, right? So how do you know about it? I don't mean just you, but how does anyone know about it since it happened that long ago?

Anyway, I was just thinking I'm kind of like that planet. I was on one path, and something knocked me onto a new one. I'm still going.

Iris

Bennie walked with us to the exit when the ship docked in Cape Oliver. None of us said anything along the way. Grandma and I each had a small bag packed. If we didn't make it back before the ship left that afternoon, we'd have a change of clothes and our toothbrushes with us. We did pack our suitcases, even though we weren't going to haul them with us. If we had to meet the ship in San Francisco to pick up the rest of our things, we wouldn't have to take time to pack. Before we'd left the room, I put the origami whale in the front pocket of my jeans for good luck.

Hopefully we would make it back, because I wasn't ready to say goodbye to Bennie. But I had to go. A whale was pulling me off that ship and down the Pacific coast. I signed *"Thank you"* to Bennie. As we hugged I realized I was still wearing the scarf she'd lent me. I reached to pull it off as I signed, *"Yours."*

She shook her head and placed a hand on mine to stop me. *"Yours."* Then she scribbled something on the notepad before handing it back to me. *Good luck. Whatever happens, you made a great song.*

I squeezed her hand; then Grandma and I walked through the exit and onto the gangplank.

Bennie had told us how to get to the train from the ship, and pretty soon we found signs, and a crowd, to follow—a lot of cruise passengers were headed to the railway tour.

After walking a few blocks, we saw a huge black train sitting on the tracks, steam billowing from the engine. It didn't look like trains I usually saw, but more old-fashioned, like something from a black-and-white movie. A man in a blue suit and a conductor's cap stood outside the train and waved everyone aboard.

Grandma handed him our tickets, and we found seats near the front. I couldn't believe we were almost there. This was it.

It seemed to take so long for the train to fill up and get going. I was ready to just go already and get to Blue 55 before he left the bay. Maybe he'd already been there. I was afraid to check, but I had to find out if there was even a reason to go anymore.

I reminded myself then that whales can hear from so far away. Even if 55 had left the bay, he wouldn't have gone far. I'd play his song for him anyway. He'd be close enough to hear it, and know that someone out there heard him and answered. So why didn't I feel better, knowing that one way or another I'd play the song I'd made and he'd hear it?

I thought back to what Tristan said, when he reminded me that Blue 55 wasn't one of my radios.

Maybe I wasn't doing this for 55. He thought I was trying to fix the whale, to make myself feel better.

No, that wasn't it. He did have a song that no one else could tune in to, but he didn't need fixing any more than I did. I pushed the doubts aside. Of course I was doing this for him.

When I took out my phone, I noticed there wasn't much of a charge left. The night before, I'd tested the speaker once more, and left the phone plugged into it instead of plugging it into the charger. If I went through all this just to have a dead phone ruin it, I'd never get over it.

I turned off my phone to save whatever battery life was left and asked Grandma if I could check the map on hers. The tracker showed a blue dot blinking right near Lighthouse Bay, and the time of his last recorded song: just an hour ago. He'd be there soon, if he kept swimming in the same direction. But would he stay? I was literally cutting my chances of meeting him down to the minute.

My leg jiggled as I switched over to the sanctuary's website to check for news. Not much of an update, just a "Today Is the Day!" post about how some of the staff was going out in a boat soon to catch up with 55 and try to tag him.

Before handing Grandma's phone back, I checked a new email that had come in. Wendell had replied to my message.

Dear Iris,

Scientists figured out that the other giant planet used to be there because of the effect it had on everything around it. The other planets and their moons would have different orbits if there hadn't been something else that size pulling on them. Our whole solar system would be different. We wouldn't have seen Jupiter that day you were at my house because it would be in another part of the sky. Even though that planet has been gone a long time and it's really far away now, it still affects the planets it used to share space with.

Come back soon, Iris. It's not the same here without you.

Wendell

The train shuddered and lurched forward, gradually picking up speed as we rolled down the tracks along the Oregon coast. I drummed my fingers on my thighs. This was it, almost the end of my journey. Later, when the train stopped at the halfway point, we'd be just a ten-minute shuttle ride from the sanctuary.

I tried to tell myself that Blue 55 would be there at the bay or he wouldn't. There wasn't anything else I could do except show up.

Still, I was nervous. I kept trying to get a view of the landscape ahead of us, hoping to see something that looked like a train stop. Grandma put a hand on my leg to stop its bouncing. I got up and moved to the passenger car closest to the engine to get a better view and to give my jittery legs something to do.

The train climbed a hill, and when we rounded over the top, a wooden building came into view. A man wearing a khaki shirt and pants waved from the front of the building as the train slowed to a stop.

After we got off the train, Grandma asked the man where to catch the shuttle; then we followed the path in the direction he pointed.

Finally, we were almost there. Grandma took my hand and even ran a little, laughing. I'd have to think of some way to thank her for bringing me on the trip. Without her, it couldn't have happened.

When we reached an area with shops and restaurants lining the streets, a blue sign on a pole pointed the way to the shuttle stop. We were back to walking, since Grandma was out of breath from the short run.

We turned the corner to see a shuttle stop ahead of us, and a shuttle rounding the corner, driving away. I ran ahead to the bench at the stop to read the sign next to it: SHUTTLE STOP, EVERY TWENTY MINUTES.

Twenty more minutes. Then a ten-minute ride. Blue 55 would probably be tagged by then, swimming away from the sanctuary. *Train gone.*

I glanced around frantically like a shuttle map was going to appear. Maybe one of the stores knew the route, and I could hurry to the next stop, wherever that was.

Grandma pointed ahead of us and to the right. *"You can make it."*

"How? Where?"

"I'll meet you at the sanctuary. Run to that whale."

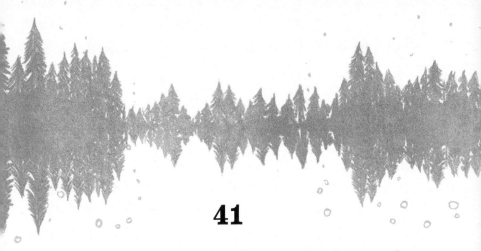

41

I tore through downtown Cape Oliver, weaving between the shops and restaurants and tourists. At a small redbrick library, I leaned against the wall to catch my breath and check once more on Blue 55.

My phone screen showed the battery life with the tiniest sliver of red. Like that line from Ms. Conn's pen, this could ruin everything. Even if I somehow made it to the sanctuary before Blue 55 left, I might not be able to play the song. All that work I put into it and all the distance I'd traveled to get there could be worthless because I hadn't plugged in my phone overnight. I'd never forgive myself for that.

Nothing I could do about it now. I'd have to just get to the sanctuary and see what happened. Until then, I'd save whatever life the phone had left. I shoved it into my sweatshirt pocket and turned in a circle, trying to figure out which way to go. I'd run the way Grandma had pointed from the shuttle stop, but a straight shot wasn't possible with all the buildings in the way. The main street was on a diagonal, so I wasn't sure if I was heading the right way or running parallel to where I'd been.

I ran again in a direction that felt right, while picturing the map that Bennie had shown us. The sanctuary was farther down the coast, I knew that much. Finally I found the beach, but couldn't see the train tracks from here to help me figure out where I was. What if I ran in the wrong direction? By the time I figured it out, I'd be even farther away from Blue 55. I touched the compass on my necklace, tracing the outline of the whale, wishing 55 could somehow show me how to reach him.

Then I smacked myself on the forehead. What I needed was hanging right there around my neck. I laughed at myself as I unclasped the necklace and opened the compass. Mr. Gunnar was right—it still worked. I'd navigate like people did for centuries. The compass needle pointed north. I turned so that north was at my back, and ran.

When I got close to the sanctuary, I didn't need a map or compass to tell me I'd found the right place. I put the compass in my sweatshirt pocket next to my phone as I ran toward the red roof of a lighthouse.

If I got there before the boat left, maybe I could convince them to change their minds about the song. I'd play it for them and show them how easy it'd be to just toss the speaker into the water. It could wait until after they tagged him so it wouldn't interfere with his song as they listened for him. It was okay that I couldn't get on the boat. I'd wait inside the building and watch the tagging on the video screens. Or I could stand outside and maybe get a glimpse of him as he swam in the bay. The important thing was that Blue 55 would hear his song.

An orange boat that looked like the one in the video from last year when Andi tried to tag 55 was in the water. Ahead of me was a jetty, with large rocks on either side like ones I'd seen in Galveston. That would get me farther into the bay.

After a few steps along the jetty, I slowed my pace. Waves crashed over the rocks and splashed onto the surface, slippery with seawater and algae. Twice I fell on the way to the end. The orange boat was ahead of me on the left, heading toward the sanctuary building. Was Blue 55 somewhere nearby, or were they going back because the expedition had failed again? Or maybe they'd already tagged him. When they got close enough, I'd flag them down. I peeled off my sweatshirt and dropped it onto the jetty with my backpack. After the run, I needed to cool off.

I started to wave as the boat got closer to me; then I lowered my hand. Andi and the man behind the wheel were both smiling. Andi held the tagging pole, which no longer had a tracker at the end. The man took one hand off the wheel to give Andi a high-five.

They were celebrating. They'd tagged the whale. Blue 55, the reason I was standing there. I'd left home to fly and cruise and ride a train and run to him, and he was gone.

I tried to be happy for Andi and her team. They had set out to tag Blue 55, and they'd done it. But I couldn't feel happy, not yet. For the first time since I started the trip, I cried. It wasn't the kind of cry that was for one thing, but the kind that brings up everything sad or unfair that ever happened.

It was possible to miss someone you'd never met. I'd come all this way because I felt alone, and thought Blue 55 did too. Alone, even in a crowd. And now he was swimming away from me. There I was, completely alone, standing in cold wet clothes on a jetty. I thought back to what the captain had said during the fjord tour. *Sometimes you have to know when it's time to give up and turn back.*

I shook my head and wiped my face. No. This couldn't be the end. I wasn't ready to give up yet. Blue 55 hadn't given up, after all those decades of singing with no one answering him. If he had, I wouldn't know about him. I wouldn't have been on that cruise ship.

There had to be something more to do, some hope to grab on to.

Blue 55 wasn't so far away yet. I wouldn't see him up close, but wasn't I doing this for him? Maybe Tristan had been right all along, and I was really doing this for myself. I was the one who was lonely, and I'd wanted the whale to hear me. But right then, all I wanted was to let him know I heard him, that he'd connected to someone. The song I'd made wouldn't be exactly like his, but it was as close as I could get. Everything I'd done would be worth it if just a few notes of the song touched his heart. I'd show him that there was at least one place in the ocean where he could find music like his own.

Wherever he was he'd still be close enough to hear his song. I grabbed the waterproof speaker from my backpack and plugged the wire into my phone. The red line showing the battery life was thinner than a hair. I tossed the thermos into the water, for the song to play as long as it would.

If I could catch sight of Blue 55 for a second, I'd have that to hang on to. I'd come for so much more, but at least I'd have something. A glimpse of his back or tail or breath right then would be like the hum of radio static against my hand. Even if I didn't feel his music, I'd know I'd gotten really close.

I scanned the waters all around the bay, back and forth, frantic. Flat waters, with the kind of stillness that must have been quiet. *Just let me see you. Let me know this wasn't all for nothing.*

No, not nothing. I touched the origami whale in my jeans pocket. At least I'd brought Grandma to the sea, and it washed away the drizzly November in her soul. She'd navigated her way through her grief. My weird, funny grandma, never content to stay in one place, who knew from the start that I should have the name of a whale. She'd never be an ordinary grandma. She was the kind who would take your hand and join you on an adventure, who had to break free like those bubbles trapped under the glacial ice. Life would never be the same without Grandpa, but we'd be all right. Grandma knew that now too.

And I'd made a good friend. I hoped we'd make it back to the *Siren* before it left port so I'd have more time with Bennie.

I'd missed seeing the whale. This whale who I knew without even meeting him, from the time I first learned his name. He'll never know that someone out there felt that way about him. Maybe he wouldn't have understood anyway, but I would have liked to have told him.

I'm sorry. I did everything I could. I'm here now.

Then I saw it, out in the waters ahead. A gray-blue whale, swimming toward me. Maybe it was another whale. There was no way to tell from where I stood on the dock.

But then, after a column of spray from the blow spout, the whale's back arched. The crescent of the dorsal fin rose above the surface, followed by the broad fluke.

There she blows.

And there, I jumped.

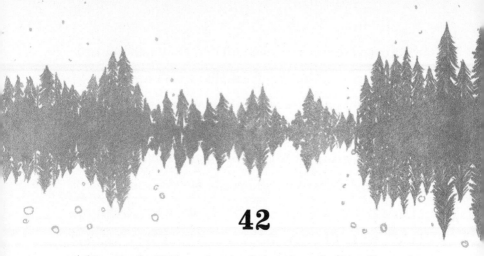

42

Cold water knifed my face as I dove into the bay. For as long as possible, I stayed under the surface, pushing through the water while aiming for the spot where I'd seen 55's blow spout.

My lungs screamed for me to breathe. I lifted my head for just a second and inhaled like I'd never get another breath, then ducked below the surface again. With eyes wide I scanned the waters around me for Blue 55.

I kicked the water, reaching for a growing shadow ahead, not stopping until the whale was right in front of me.

This wasn't how I'd planned to meet him, but it was happening. No picture I'd ever seen could compare to seeing the whale up close. He didn't seem quite real before, when he was just an image on a screen or a photo on my wall. I floated in the bay, staring into the whale's dark eye, impossibly small for such a huge animal. No bigger than the palm of my hand. But when I gazed into its depths, it was like 55 was showing me everything he'd ever felt and everything he'd ever seen.

He stared back. Was there recognition there? A connection? Did he have any idea how far I'd come for him?

It didn't matter anymore. We were there, together. I'd found him. He'd never know what he meant to me, but that was okay. I didn't speak his language, and he didn't need to be fixed. He was the whale who sang his own song.

We circled, studying each other. I surfaced to take a breath. The orange boat from the tagging expedition was headed in our direction. I'd have to join them soon, but I wasn't ready to leave the whale I'd been chasing for so long.

Blue 55 wouldn't need to breathe again, maybe not for another twenty minutes. He waited, hovering beside me, each time I surfaced. We were almost close enough to touch, but maybe he'd want to keep some distance. He didn't swim away; just glided around me, keeping his eye on mine. I held out my hand. Those waters were his home, and I was a guest. I'd traveled more than four thousand miles to meet Blue 55. The last few feet would be up to him.

He drifted closer, closing the gap between us, until his face brushed my fingertips. I slid my open hand alongside his body, the dark gray-blue skin. His parents had given him their colors but neither could give him their language. So he made his own.

And I'd have just a moment to share mine with his. I rested my hand on his side, then tapped out his name.

55, 55, 55.

You're a poem, did you know that?

A new poem came to me then, just as easily as if Grandpa were there signing it with me. I kept my hands in the five handshape but closed the fingers together. A good shape for ocean waves and music.

Your music sailed through the ocean
and over the land
and carried me here.
Sing your song.

I will never write down the poem. It belonged to this whale, and I'll leave it here in the sea, where it will live in the space above and below and all around him.

43

He remembered a time, one he'd tried so hard to forget. A time before he knew the loneliness.

The song he'd ached for, had searched for in the world's seas, was here. Calls like his own filled the waters around him. He didn't know this place, but the feeling it gave him, one deep in his memory, told him he was home.

The whale dove down and rose up and reclaimed every song he'd ever created and abandoned on the waves. He sang them all, right then, in a bellow of music that ripped through the ocean.

And after all the years of calling and searching, after so much time and loneliness, so many calls left unheard and unanswered, the whale thought that maybe, finally, someone was listening.

44

Sound can move anything if it's strong enough.

The bellowing song of Blue 55 traveled through me so strongly that my body vibrated like one big radio speaker. Of all the sounds in the world, this one had to be the most beautiful. I knew that without ever having heard a thing. I'd made a song for him, and he gave me his own right back. I wished I could stay right there forever, where I'd always feel the waves of that music.

The cold and the need for air were the only things that could tear me away. I grabbed for the surface, while 55's music still rippled the water. He swam back to me, nudging my side like he was making sure I was okay.

We surfaced together, then swam toward the boat. I raised my hand to wave.

Andi stood up near the front. She pointed at me as she said something to the driver. Then she turned to me, and her mouth formed the question "Iris?"

I nodded and smiled, even though I was shivering. The man tossed me a life preserver. Before grabbing on for them to pull me aboard, I rested a palm on the side of the whale's face to tell him goodbye.

Keep singing, Blue 55.

As the boat drove us toward the sanctuary building, I was thinking the cold water must have frozen my brain. It looked like my parents were waiting for me on the dock.

Frozen as I was, I wasn't hallucinating. My parents stood there, arms around each other, on the dock in front of the sanctuary, along with Grandma. I braced myself for them to lecture me about the Serious Trouble I was in. But they didn't. Certainly it would come, but they were holding it for later. Dad was the first one to wrap me in a hug.

When he let go I stepped back so he could see me. With shivering hands I signed, *"I didn't miss the boat."*

"Or the train," he added. He put his coat around me and led me inside.

"Sorry for everything," I told him. *"Am I grounded for life?"*

He nodded. *"Maybe longer."*

Totally worth it.

"Make a splash" is another figure of speech I understand better now. Usually it means to make a strong impression and to get a lot of attention. Thankfully I did make a big splash when I jumped into the water, because it caught the attention of a man on a nearby dock. He flagged down Andi and pointed me out. I didn't remember screaming when I hit the water, but apparently I did that, too.

After my email to Mom asking her not to blame Grandma for our trip, my parents had guessed that I'd gone looking for the whale. My postcard from Alaska was a bigger clue. All they had to do then was search online for news about Blue 55. They got on a plane to Oregon and drove to Lighthouse Bay, where they met Andi.

My punishment would wait until we got home. For now, they just wanted to see me and know that I was all right. And I was. Grandma and I would head back to the ship to finish the cruise, then fly home together. We promised not to take any detours.

Mom didn't say much; she mostly just held me. Now and then she pulled away to brush back my damp hair and look at me like she was making sure I was really there, before holding me again like she'd never let go. I hugged her back to let her know that was okay with me.

Andi brought me another cup of hot chocolate. That helped to warm me up, along with Dad's coat and the blankets the staff gave me. While my clothes dried I'd changed into a sanctuary T-shirt and a pair of pajama pants I had packed, after we picked up my backpack from the jetty.

I did get that tour Andi had promised, even though we weren't at her sanctuary in Appleton. The staff let her show me around and introduce me to all those animals I'd seen on the website. Computer screens in one of the offices showed graphs with wavy lines that moved up and down. They looked like the graphs I'd seen in articles about whale songs. Andi pointed out the labels for each one, showing where the hydrophones were that picked up whale songs. A line on the last graph moved up and down close to the line labeled "55 Hertz." Blue 55's graph, showing that he was singing.

Andi slid a notepad between us and wrote, *Have you thought about what you'll be when you're older?*

I shrugged. I'd always figured I'd do something with electronics but wasn't sure what that would be, what I'd do every day for a job.

All of this—Andi pointed to the computer screens—

and what you did with the song is called acoustic biology.
People in that field study sounds that animals make when
communicating.

I could work with sound. And whales. Like those scientists I'd read about who studied whale songs to make migration maps. I learned the song of this whale, and I will learn it for others.

Andi added, *You'd be good at it,* then crossed it out. Beneath that she wrote *You're good at it.*

Before we left the sanctuary, Dad held my hand as we stood at the window to watch Blue 55 swim throughout the bay. He would stay, or he would move on. After swimming in warmer waters for the winter, maybe he'd come back here, to this place where he'd heard his song. And he'd remember a girl who swam with him when it first played.

He and Mara, the young blue whale, might learn to communicate with each other, just a little. As she grew older Mara would look and sound more like his mother. They didn't speak the same language, but once in a while, one of them might say the right thing. They'd have that much. And that would be worth coming back for.

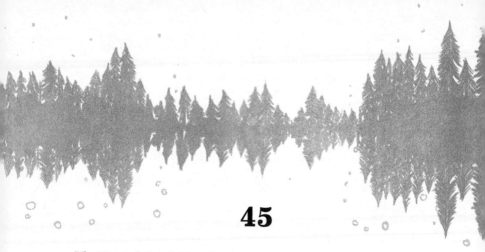

45

The first thing I did when I got back to school was hurry to Sofia Alamilla's room. I had to make it quick so I wouldn't be late to Ms. Conn's class. Everyone kept waving and trying to talk to me in the halls, which slowed me down.

As soon as she saw me, she stopped writing on the board and grabbed me in a tight hug. Everything I'd thought to say to her disappeared. How could I explain what she'd done for me? If she hadn't shown the Blue 55 documentary, I wouldn't have known about him. We wouldn't have found each other. He'd still be out there on his own, not knowing anyone heard him. And I wouldn't know that anyone heard me.

Sorry for missing so much school, I wrote on the board. *I'll catch up. Thank you so much for teaching me about Blue 55.*

I'm so happy you're all right, she wrote. *I hope you found what you were looking for.*

I started to write that yes, I'd found the whale and played the song for him. But Ms. Alamilla knew that. By then, the news had spread about where I'd been. She must have meant something more than the whale.

Yes, I did. I gave her another quick hug before running off to Ms. Conn's class.

Nina signed *"Welcome back"* as I slid into the room, and it wasn't that horrible. At the last second I dropped into my chair, and Mr. Charles and I signed together *"By a hair."*

So much had happened in the time I'd been gone, but I could count on Ms. Conn and her pickle face to never change.

Ms. Conn gave us time to work on our reports during class. And I needed it, with all the catching up I had to do. Since I knew so much more about whales than I had just a week earlier, I thought the report would be easy to write. Then I found there was so much to say about them, it was hard to decide where to start. I took out my notes and added what I'd learned from Sura about bubble net feeding.

As I wrote about whale communication, I kept thinking about Grandpa and what he'd told me about the sei whale that day on the beach. *A whale can't find its way through a world without sound.... But it's different for us....*

Mr. Charles tapped my desk. When I looked up he signed, *"Are you thinking about whales or something else?"*

"Both," I answered. *"Whales, and my grandpa."*

Mr. Charles smiled. *"What would he say about the trip you took with your grandma?"*

On the flight home Grandma had asked if I'd thought about talking to my mom about going to Bridgewood. I wondered what made her think of it then. The trip didn't have anything to do with that. Did it? I didn't like the way my stomach felt when I thought about going to a new school with new people, even though we'd share a language.

Grandpa had told me I would find my way, even though it might take time to figure things out. Maybe finding your way sometimes means you can't stay where you are.

"Grandpa would want me to do for myself what I did for the whale."

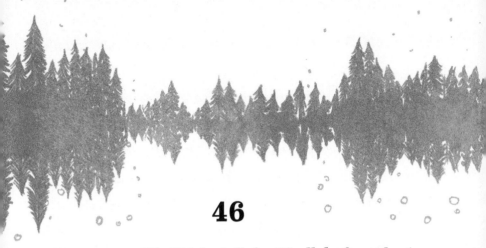

46

"She is responsible. Think of all she did, all she figured out on her own!"

Grandma was in the living room talking to Mom. I'd called her and told her I'd been thinking about what we'd discussed on the plane. I did want to go to Bridgewood. From the upstairs game room, I had a view of the conversation if I peeked through the railing.

"Sure, she shouldn't have taken off like that. The whale song moved her so much she couldn't help herself." Grandma didn't sign *"move"* as in moving from one place to another, though the song did that too. She touched her heart.

Mom wiped her eyes with a tissue Grandma handed her. *"I always felt so left out, the way you and Dad could talk to each other, the connection you had with your Deaf friends. Like you have with Iris now."*

"I'm sorry," Grandma signed. *"We didn't mean to leave*

you out. And no one means to leave Iris out, either. But it's happening."

"I don't want to lose her if she's around other Deaf people all the time. She won't need me anymore."

"She'll always need her mom. She's already lost, spending every day with people she can't talk to. Don't you think Iris wishes she could see that whale every day? But she didn't try to drag him back here to live with her. She helped him feel more at home."

Mom didn't argue with that. It seemed like the conversation was winding down, so I backed away from the railing and went to my room, where Mom found me a few minutes later.

"Grandma thinks you want to go to Bridgewood." She looked like she was trying to laugh a little, as if she wanted to add, "Isn't that ridiculous?" She also looked nauseated.

There was my chance to back out, to pretend that it was some crazy idea of Grandma's. I'd already hurt Mom so much.

But then everything would go back to like it was before. All day, every school day, with no one but Mr. Charles to talk to. The thought of going to a school where I'd know hardly anyone was scary, but it was better than the dread I'd feel about spending my next years of school like the last ones. If Blue 55 could find happiness hanging out at the sanctuary with animals he'd never met, I could be happy at a new school.

I set aside the electronics parts I was pretending to organize, and sat on my bed next to Mom. The origami whale was perched on my nightstand, worse for the wear from the swim in the bay. Grandma had remade it for me on the plane after I'd unfolded it to let it dry. She offered to make a new one on paper that wasn't faded and blurred, but I wanted to keep the one she'd made on the ship, the one that was with me when I met Blue 55.

After a deep breath I told Mom, *"I do want to go. I want to be around other Deaf kids like Wendell. People who speak my language."*

"I speak your language," she answered.

"I know, and I'm really happy you do. And that Dad . . . sort of does. But you don't have to unless you decide to. You know it's different for Deaf people. I can't keep going through the school day all alone."

"I think it'll be hard for you, starting over with so many new people."

"Every day is hard."

Mom rested her head in her hands, and I leaned over to put my arm around her. I tapped her leg so she'd look at me again. Even though it might give away that I was watching the conversation downstairs, I told her, *"You'll never lose me. I'll always need my mom."*

47

I opened a chat window and found Wendell online.

Guess what? I typed.

You hitched a ride on an African safari and you've befriended a cheetah.

Close, I answered. *I'm going to Bridgewood next year.*

Wow, really? That's awesome! So you finally talked to your mom.

Yeah. She still doesn't like the idea, but she said okay. I'm going to be nervous, though. I'll hardly know anyone.

Yeah, unlike where you are now, most popular student, class president, and all that.

I sat back and laughed. If Wendell were there, I'd throw a pillow at his head.

So how grounded are you? he asked.

Forever.

See if your parents will let you stop by sometime, he added. *My mom said I could invite you over for dinner to welcome you home. I think she was worried while you were gone, so she wants to see you too.*

Okay, I'll try. Any cool planet sightings or eclipses to see?

Not this week. But I'm pretty cool, so you should come over anyway.

Good enough. I'll stop by whenever my parents let me out of their sight.

I was elbow-deep in a radio when Tristan came in. "Ready to go?"

"Almost," I signed with the leather gloves still on. Really, the radio would take a lot more time, and some parts I didn't have yet. I'd take it back to Mr. Gunnar after fixing it. Probably.

Tristan helped me straighten up my workbench and put things away. I let him, even though he didn't know where to put everything. He set the radio on an empty spot on a high shelf I pointed out for him. The repair would wait for another day. Time to take Grandma to the beach.

Grandma and I walked the dunes to pick wildflowers for the grave of Iris the sei whale. I filled her in on how Blue 55 was doing. His tracker app showed he was still hanging

around the sanctuary, though he'd swim away sometimes and return later. Andi had forwarded a recording of the song I'd made to the staff there, and talked to
the acoustic biologists about how interesting it would
be to find out how Blue 55 responded to it. Through an
underwater speaker in the bay, they played his song
sometimes. Other sanctuaries along his route would do
the same, when he swam in their waters.

An update on the Lighthouse Bay website said that
he'd visited all the sea pens. Sometimes he and Mara
swam together. How long would he stay? Would he
return to the sanctuary every year? It was impossible
to know, but it'd be fun to find out what happened.

Grandma squeezed my hand. *"You did a good thing.
Thank you so much for going on the adventure with me. It
was exactly what I needed. Even though Grandpa wasn't
around to enjoy it, I feel like he's with me again. I think
when I was that sad, there wasn't any room for him. Now
there is."*

Then she told me about her new home.

"What?" I replied. *"A cruise ship? Full-time? How?"*
I didn't know people could do that. Apparently she'd
been looking into it. Not many people lived on cruise
ships year-round, but it was possible.

"You saw how happy I was. I'll be at sea all the time. It doesn't cost much more than Oak Manor. It's just for a year. Then I'll decide what to do."

A year. So many days without Grandma around.

"Do you know my favorite quote from Moby-Dick*?"* she asked. *"It's not the one about the drizzly November in the soul, though I like that one too. 'It is not down on any map; true places never are.' Where we traveled together isn't on any map, and I'll get to keep it with me all the time."*

The wildflowers we'd left on the whale's grave rolled across the sand when a gust of wind blew. I rearranged them and stuck the stems into the sand while I thought about what to say. Grandma couldn't leave. Yes, she'd been really happy on the cruise. But a whole year away from us?

She tapped me so I'd look at her again. *"And this way your mother won't worry about me wandering off. Not far to go on a ship."*

"Is this because of what I said in Skagway?" I asked. *"About living on a ship if you had a big win at the casino? You know I was kidding, right?"*

She nodded. *"I know. But after what I've done, how could I stay? Think about what it'll be like."* She held up a hand, two fingers pointed at her own face.

I lifted my hands to argue with her, then let them

drop to the sand. She was right. They'd never take their eyes off her.

A few days later an envelope from Bennie arrived in the mail. She'd emailed to ask how I was doing and to get my home address so she could send me something. Inside the envelope were some photos of the cruise. One was of Bennie and me sitting on deck together, in a photo I hadn't noticed the photographer taking. I looked happy. In another that was taken from the deck below, I was by myself looking out over the water. I'd probably been wondering where 55 was and if I'd find him.

I'd give Grandma the picture of the two of us, from our first day on the cruise. She could keep it with her while she sailed to wherever she'd be during the next year.

The last picture was of Grandma performing in the karaoke bar. I tacked it to my wall. Whenever I felt sad about Grandma being away, the photo would remind me that she was where she needed to be. Not a place on any map.

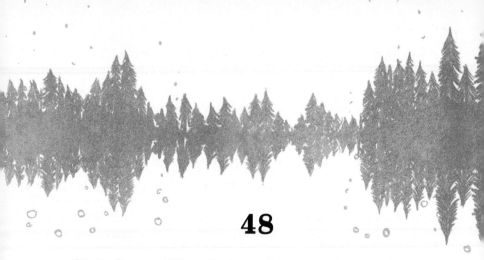

48

Ms. Jackson said I could ride with her and Wendell to school. I'd do that most days, but for my first day at Bridgewood Junior High, Mom wanted to drive me.

She parked at the curb and waited while I sat there looking out the window at all the students heading into the school. Was this what I wanted? I didn't know any of those people.

But I could. I hadn't known anyone at my old school either, not really. Here, I'd have a chance.

Mom touched my arm. *"You know you can always change your mind,"* she signed after I looked at her.

"I know," I signed, even though I wouldn't change my mind.

She smiled and pointed toward the front door of the school. I turned to see Wendell, wearing his "I Need My Space" Saturn shirt and waving to me from the top of the steps.

I laughed and leaned over to hug Mom. She held me like she didn't want to let go but would do it anyway. As soon as I sat back, I threw out an *"I love you,"* beating her to it.

"You're going to do great," she signed as I opened the door.

Across the street was the elementary school, where Mr. Charles would be working. Knowing he was nearby helped me miss him a little less.

Before walking up the steps, I turned back to wave goodbye to Mom. But she wasn't looking at me. She was watching a group of Deaf students standing under a tree. I wondered what she was thinking as they hugged and signed to one another. Maybe she was seeing what I'd be able to have, what I'd be a part of now. Even though she wouldn't see me, I waved goodbye to her, then started up the steps to my new school.

A sound can move anything if it's strong enough. It can shake walls or break glass. It can knock a whale onto a new path. It can pick someone up and carry her far from home where she doesn't know anyone. The vibration of the whale song would stay with me always.

Blue 55 had found a new home. Maybe some friends. I would too.

AUTHOR'S NOTE

Whale Communication and the 52-Hertz Whale

The whale in this novel is fictitious but is based on the real 52-hertz whale, also known as the Loneliest Whale in the World and 52 Blue. As of this writing, no one has met him and he does not wear a tracker. He's known only because of his unusual song. Some marine biologists hypothesize that he is either malformed in some way or is a hybrid of two species of whale. When I learned about the 52-hertz whale, I wondered about what life was like for a whale that sang like no other, and wished I could find out how he was doing.

Maybe one day someone will track down the 52-hertz whale, and we'll learn more about him and why he sings the way he does. For this story, the whale is made up of the few characteristics we know for certain about 52 Blue, plus my own imagination and what I learned from researching whales. But I also gave him a different identity. By fictionalizing the whale, I had the freedom to create his story, physical description, and song pattern. I chose the fifty-five-hertz frequency since it's close to the real whale's sound and because the repeated "five" in his name ties in with the sign language poetry in the story. Blue 55 is a hybrid of a blue and a fin whale, the world's two largest whale species. Though hybrid whales are rare, these two baleen whales are closely related enough to reproduce, and there have been a few known blue-fin hybrids.

We are able to hear the song of 52 Blue, and all whales, because of underwater microphones, or hydrophones. A hydrophone system originally used for the US military to detect enemy submarines was made available to marine biologists in the late 1980s. By using the equipment to listen to whale songs, scientists can identify and track species of whales in the oceans. In 1989, scientist William Watkins of Woods Hole Oceanographic Institution (WHOI) noticed one whale song in the North Pacific Ocean that didn't sound like any other. In some ways, the song sounded like those of blue and fin whales, with short and frequent calls. But the frequency was much higher: fifty-two hertz instead of the normal fifteen to twenty-five hertz. For humans, it's a low sound—like the lowest note a tuba can play—but it's a high one for blue and fin whales. The song would continue sometimes for hours before stopping as abruptly as it had started. For the next twelve years, Watkins and his team recorded the extraordinary song from fall to late winter, when the whale swam out of range of the hydrophones.

In addition to having a unique song, this whale has an unusual migration route. While most whales visit the same areas each year, the 52-hertz whale's path varies from one year to the next. Some years he travels much farther north or west than others, and at times he has meandering routes, wandering up and down the Pacific coast. He can swim up to forty-two miles a day, and the presence or absence of other whales doesn't seem to affect where he travels.

Of course, it's impossible to know whether or not 52 Blue is actually a "lonely whale." Another scientist who has recorded him, whale communication expert Christopher Clark of Cornell University, said in a 2015 BBC interview, "The animal's singing with a lot of the same features of a typical blue whale song. Blue whales, fin whales, and humpback whales: all these whales can hear this guy; they're not deaf. He's just odd." Dr. Clark also points out that other unusual whale calls have been recorded, and some whale populations have their own regional dialects.

Though the WHOI researchers found that the 52-hertz song was coming from only one source, more recent recordings suggest that there could be more than one whale calling at that frequency. Data from John Hildebrand of the Scripps Institution of

Oceanography shows similar calls off the California coast, in locations too far apart to have come from the same animal. Perhaps there is a small population of whales who sing at this high frequency.

The song of the 52-hertz whale has changed over the years, steadily growing lower. Whether from ocean noise or his own maturity or some other reason, he now sings at a frequency of about forty-seven hertz.

He isn't alone in changing his song. Some whale species, like humpbacks and bowheads, add new "verses" to their songs each season, sometimes picking up parts of songs from other groups of whales they encounter. Perhaps the musical complexity makes them more desirable to potential mates, or perhaps they just enjoy singing new songs. Some whale communication changes out of necessity. Noise pollution in the ocean has led some whales to change their songs over time. With constant ship traffic and oil drilling, the ocean is far noisier than it used to be. Much like people talking loudly to be heard in a noisy room, the whales have to adjust their sounds to hear one another over the other noise in the ocean.

We might never know what whales are saying, but we can keep listening.

DEAFNESS & SIGN LANGUAGE

Around the time 52 Blue was discovered, I was discovering sign language. As a psychology major, I wasn't planning to get into the field of interpreting, but I took a sign language course as an elective. Then I took another. At the time, those two courses were all the college offered, but I wasn't finished. I started taking sign language courses taught by Deaf people, outside of school. At the end of each six-week course, I signed up for the next, and our small class would pick up where we'd left off last time. I continued that for about a year and a half, and started interpreting for some of the college's Deaf students during my last semester as a student. I moved out of state after graduating, but I knew I wasn't leaving sign language behind. What had started out as a fun elective would turn into a career and a never-ending education. My first interpreting jobs after college were in public schools, and I continued to learn more and more from sign language workshops and the Deaf people I met.

I was surprised to meet so many Deaf people whose families never learned sign language, or never learned it very well. Unlike Iris, most Deaf people do not have others like them in their families. Most deafness isn't hereditary, so about 90 percent of Deaf children are born to hearing parents, who are unlikely to know sign language. Especially in areas without a high deaf population, the sign language interpreter is often a student's only exposure to sign language and the only adult the student can communicate with.

The character of Iris came to me as the kind of person who'd be compelled to track down the lonely whale, since she's one of the many kids who go through every day feeling like she isn't heard. At the same time, it was important for me to write a character who would not wish to be "cured" but is comfortable with her deafness, and learns after her journey to advocate for herself about her own education and need for a community.

Like any group of people, the deaf population is a diverse one. The characters portrayed in this story communicate using American Sign Language, though not all deaf people do. Some prefer to speak and lipread only, with the help of speech therapy sessions, and use hearing aids or cochlear implants to enhance the hearing they do have. Others, like Iris, prefer not to communicate orally, especially if their deafness is profound. Many Deaf people, like Iris's grandmother, may use their speaking and lip-reading skills when communicating with people who don't sign and use sign language with other Deaf people.

Giving Iris a set of Deaf grandparents allowed me to show the language and culture they share, and their connection to one another. Without those moments of joy, readers not familiar with deafness might assume that Iris wishes she could hear. The Deaf community is a strong one, and despite the isolation and frustration its members experience because of the language barrier, most wouldn't want to change their deafness, any more than the rest of us would be willing to give up our friends, language, and culture. Like everyone, Iris does wish to feel heard, and for a place she belongs.

The title of the book that Iris finds in Ms. Jackson's classroom is fictitious, but the information she reads about sign language is true. Thomas Hopkins Gallaudet traveled to France to learn about educating deaf students, then returned to the United States with Laurent Clerc, a teacher and former student of the French school. In 1817, they founded the American School for the Deaf in Hartford, Connecticut. Deaf students from all over the country attended the school, bringing with them the signs they used in their own homes and communities. These signs, combined with the French sign language used by Clerc and Gallaudet, eventually became American Sign Language. The largest population of the school's students came from Martha's Vineyard, Massachusetts, which had such a high rate of hereditary deafness that even the hearing residents regularly used sign language.

Later, more states built boarding schools for deaf students. In these residential schools, generations of students passed along sign language and Deaf culture. Though many deaf students still attend residential schools, most are now mainstreamed with hearing students in schools close to home. Ideally, they have other deaf students and teachers to interact with, but that opportunity doesn't always exist, especially in small communities.

American Sign Language is a natural language, with its own rules and grammar, rather than an invented system to represent English visually. Like spoken languages, signed languages are created by the people who use them, and they grow and change over time. They aren't modeled after a spoken language but develop independently, from interactions among a population of people. Because of this, signed languages vary from country to country and can have a very different grammar from a country's spoken language. The signed languages of England and the United States are not at all similar, even though those countries share the spoken language of English. American Sign Language has similarities to French Sign Language, though. There are even regional differences within a country, much like accents in spoken language. As with all languages, new vocabulary is added as needed, because of technological advances, for example.

Sign language involves more than just the hands. Facial expressions are an important part of ASL grammar and can compare to "tone of voice" in a spoken language. Raised eyebrows, for example, show that the sentence being signed is a yes or no question rather than a statement. Also, the space in front of the signer is important and makes sign language three-dimensional. Signs can indicate the direction someone traveled, map out the placement of buildings, or show how two cars crashed. Changing the movement or placement of a sign can completely change the meaning.

For those interested in learning sign language, it's easier than ever to find a class. Many high schools and colleges now offer sign language courses, and there are free online video courses. The best way to learn is from Deaf people who use sign language regularly, so looking for videos in which Deaf people are demonstrating the signs will provide the most accurate model of the language.

Look for an opportunity to learn this unique language—it's fun to do, it's a great skill to have, and you might meet some new friends.

Though I've interpreted in many different settings in the twenty-plus years since I started out, I still remember those first students I interpreted for. Iris and Wendell are made up of many of the funny and smart Deaf kids I've met and admired over the years who I've seen struggle to figure out where they belong. I hope I've done them, and the lonely whale, justice with this story.

HOW TO SIGN
SONG FOR A WHALE

1.

2.

3.

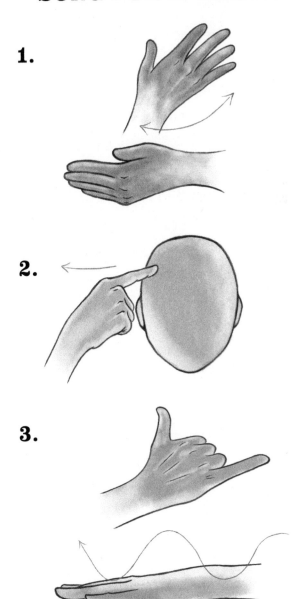

ACKNOWLEDGMENTS

A loud song of thanks and praise to everyone in the pod:

Editor Kate Sullivan at Delacorte Press for taking on the manuscript and having the vision needed to make it better. It took me just a couple days of wandering around and mumbling at the sky to see that all those revision notes made perfect sense. And to the whole Random House Children's team: editorial assistant Alexandra Hightower, art director Maria Middleton, vice president and publisher Beverly Horowitz, copyeditor Colleen Fellingham, marketing manager Hannah Black, Adrienne Waintraub and Kristin Schulz of school and library marketing, and everyone who worked to get this book into shape and into the hands of readers.

Illustrator Leo Nickolls, I couldn't have envisioned a better cover.

Literary agent Molly O'Neill of Root Literary for taking me on as a client, offering support and guidance, and finding the right home for this novel. Ten years ago, when I had my first conference critique, neither of us had any way of knowing I was sitting across from my future agent. Yet here we are, and I'm so thankful it worked out that way.

Foreign rights agent Heather Baror-Shapiro of Baror International for getting this book into the hands of readers around the world.

Dr. Amy June Rowley of California State University–East Bay and Jenna Beacom, who read the manuscript for linguistic and Deaf culture accuracy. All my years working in the sign language interpreting field couldn't give me the perspective of native signers who grew up Deaf, so I'll be forever grateful for your feedback.

Jonathan Stanley fielded my many questions about electronics and what it was like to be a "deaf radio nerd" as a kid.

Joanne Jarzobski for sharing her knowledge about the whales she loves so much. The whales are lucky to have you, as are your students.

Michael Modzelewski for answering questions about humpbacks and about being a cruise ship naturalist.

John Calambokidis of Cascadia Research Collective for helping me fix my description of a hybrid blue-fin whale and explaining how Iris would recognize Blue 55.

Sean Kelly for his knowledge of all things maritime, from local pilots to captains' pants.

Any of the book's factual errors are due to my own

oversight and not asking those experts the right questions.

I don't know how many drafts this novel went through, but there are people who've ridden along the whole journey. The Will Write for Cake critique group: Laura Edge, Doris Fisher, Miriam King, Christina Mandelski, Monica Vavra, and Tammy Waldrop. To my "Lodge of Death" writing friends, I don't know what I'd do without our retreats. Special thanks to those who read the full manuscript and helped me get it ready to submit: Samantha Clark, Shelli Cornelison, Nikki Loftin, Kayla Olson, and Corey Wright.

To Crystal Allen for having the brilliant idea to go on a writing cruise. The brainstorming at sea and feedback from Crystal and fellow cruisers Mary Beth Miller, Dixie Keyes, and Bettina Restrepo helped tie everything together (*of course* Iris has to build something to solve the problem!). Additional thanks to Bettina for answering questions about school band and orchestra.

To Katherine Applegate and Millicent Simmonds, thank you for your lovely words about Iris and her story.

My family and friends for the ongoing support and cheerleading.

Thank you all for your help in composing the song.

ABOUT THE AUTHOR

Lynne Kelly has spent twenty-five years as a sign language interpreter. Her work has taken her everywhere, from classrooms to hospitals to Alaskan cruises. Her first novel, the award-winning *Chained,* was named to seven state reading lists and won the SCBWI's Crystal Kite Award. She lives in Houston, Texas, with her adorable dog, Holly. *Song for a Whale* is her second novel.